39 (83)

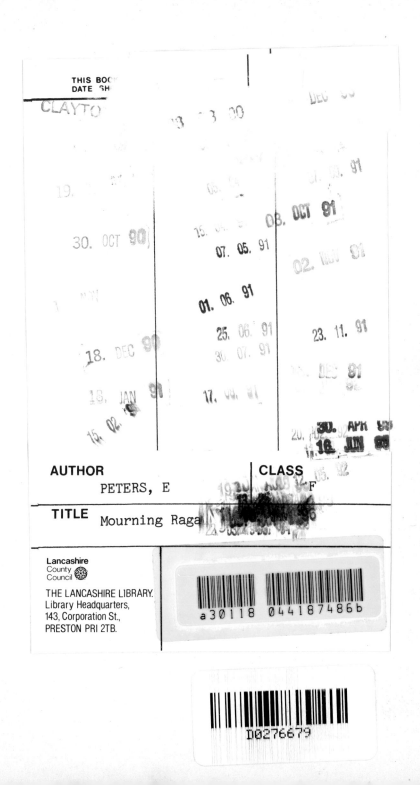

AUTHOR

    PETERS, E

CLASS

F

TITLE Mourning Raga

MOURNING RAGA

MOURNING RAGA

Ellis Peters

HEADLINE

Copyright © 1972 Ellis Peters

First published in 1972
by Macmillan London Ltd

First published in paperback in 1988
by HEADLINE BOOK PUBLISHING PLC

First published in this edition in 1990
by HEADLINE BOOK PUBLISHING PLC

04418748

British Library Cataloguing in Publication Data

Peters, Ellis, *1913–*
Mourning raga.
Rn: Edith Pargeter   I. Title
823'.912 [F]

ISBN 0–7472–0231–1

Printed and bound in Great Britain by
Richard Clay Ltd, Bungay, Suffolk

HEADLINE BOOK PUBLISHING PLC
Headline House,
79 Great Titchfield Street
London W1P 7FN

I

The whole affair began, as the unexpected and chaotic so often did, with Tossa's mother. And as usual, on the telephone.

Tossa's mother was herself unexpected and chaotic, though contained in as neat and trim a package as you could wish, slim and brown and perennially young, even after three marriages and two widowhoods. She had begun life – indeed, she still continued it, with unflagging verve and success – as Chloe Bliss, a perfect name for the stage though it also happened to be her own by the grace of fate; had been in succession Chloe Barber, until Tossa's professor father inconsiderately died in his charming prime, Chloe Terrell, until the infinitely less interesting and less suitable Herbert Terrell fell off a mountain in Slovakia and got the worst of it in the consequent collision with a slab of white trias limestone, and Chloe Newcombe, which after two years, rather surprisingly, she still was. Perhaps Paul Newcombe, on the face of it a depressingly solid and stolid type of business manipulator, was more durable than he looked; perhaps, even, there was more to him than met the eye. If he was to hold Chloe's vagrant interest much longer there would certainly need to be.

The enchanting creature who was such a problem to her husbands was no less a headache to her daughter, with the rueful difference that there was only one daughter, and she could never shuck off the load on to a successor. It was late now for Chloe to produce a co-custodian, even if she did still look no more than thirty. In lieu of a son she had cheerfully set up a stake in a prospective son-in-law. In any case, Chloe could never resist putting on her maximum charm for any young man who was drawn into her orbit. Usually they succumbed; in Dominic Felse's case she was

5

content to play it as a delicious game, and close her devastating purple-brown eyes to the consideration of whether she was winning or losing. After all, Miss Theodosia Barber was her daughter, and in her complex and evasive heart Chloe had a natural love for her, and – even better – a very healthy and wary respect.

They were in Tossa's rooms in a genteelly decaying corner of north Oxford when the call came through, and Dominic's recently-acquired third-hand Mini was sitting at the kerb outside, waiting to take them down for the Christmas vacation. They were looking forward to a peaceful celebration in the bosom of his family, and privately congratulating themselves on the fact that Chloe was frantically filming, well behind schedule, somewhere in Somerset, and hardly likely to give a thought to her daughter's activities while the panic lasted. Conscience prompted her to manifest mother-love from time to time, with an overexuberance which was designed to make up for the long neglects in between; but conscience knew better than to interfere with business. Consequently the maternal interludes usually came when they could do the most devastating damage to Tossa's plans, and none whatsoever to Chloe's.

The phone rang in the hall below. Across the case on which Dominic was kneeling they looked sharply and speculatively at each other. Dominic's left eyebrow elevated itself dubiously. He said: 'Uh-huh!' in a tone Tossa was inclined to resent, though she herself frequently said very much more on the same subject.

'It may not be for me,' she said, convincing nobody.

But it was for her. Her landlady's voice called up to her with the promptness of a derisive echo, and she went down resignedly to fend off the inevitable. Distant and guarded, gruffer than usual with defensive tension, her miniature baritone eddied up the staircase:

'Tossa Barber here – Oh, yes ... hullo, Mother! How are you? How is the shooting going?' Side-track her back into her proper sphere, that was the strategy; but Chloe

6

could always talk twice as sweetly and three times as fast. 'Yes, well, darling, you know we were going up to Midshire ...'

Were going! Dominic stopped wrestling with the recalcitrant lock of Tossa's big case, and conveyed himself across the room and halfway down the stairs in a hurry, to a position where he could sit and brood balefully over the conversation, and make entirely sure that his interests were not forgotten. Every time she raised her eyes she could not help but see him, shamelessly listening and willing her to harden her heart. Chloe had a particularly annoying way of erupting just when they were all set for a holiday.

Computing the total content of a telephone conversation from one end of it, and the passive end at that, is never easy. With a kingfisher mind like Chloe's at the far end of the line it was next door to impossible.

'Yes, I remember you said she had ... terribly interesting! Oh, really! Well, but what can I ...' A long interval of the distant purring, while Tossa's eyes took on a stunned and glazed look first of shock and then of total non-comprehension. Something fearful was going on. Dominic loomed threateningly, and she flashed him a helpless glance and shook her head at him to show she hadn't forgotten everything they had arranged between them. '*Where?* But ... No, but you're serious? I ... well, of course I do see how marvellous, but ... So *far*! And I'd be scared, alone! Oh! ... Oooohh!' she breathed in a long, awakening sigh, and a gleam came to life, far behind the glassy astonishment of her eyes, and grew and grew, like a moonrise. A hint of excited colour flicked her cheeks. Drat the girl, she was falling for it, whatever *it* was, after all her years of experience with that infuriating, lovely mother of hers. Dominic shuffled his feet and cleared his throat menacingly, and Tossa looked up and smiled at him with the eerie bliss of a sleepwalker. 'But would she really ... for *both* of us? Well, of course, I do realise it's a once-in-a-lifetime chance ... But, gosh, Mother, I don't know! I *would* love

7

to ... I bet he would, too ... Look, let me talk to him and call you back ...'

'Yes,' said Dominic grimly, just too quietly to be heard at the other end, 'you do that! Get her off there and give *me* a chance to get some sense into you. *That Chloe!*'

'A quarter of an hour, Mother, yes, I promise. Give me that number again ...'

She cradled the receiver and came drifting up the stairs muttering it to herself, and Dominic gave her his ball-pen to write it down, before she lost herself among the digits. She looked a little drunk, on what manner of intoxicant he couldn't imagine. *She* was usually the one who had all the evasions ready when Chloe sent out distress signals. She, after all, could be as cynical as she liked about her own mother; Dominic knew better than to venture on the same terms. He had an instinct for the exact line where his privilege ran out, and he was light on his feet, and could always stop short of it. He took her by the hand and towed her back into her own room. Her knees gave under her; she sat down dreamily on the bed, staring through him into the pale December sky.

'Now, look, we were going to my parents in Comerford, remember?' Help, she'd got him talking in the wrong tense now! 'We *are* going!'

'Yes, of course! I haven't forgotten anything. If you say so, when you know ... if *they* say so, that's where we're going. I wouldn't ditch them for anybody in the world. You know that. But wait till I tell you what she offered us ...'

'Us!' Yes, give her that, Tossa had made sure that he was included.

'It isn't what you think, she doesn't want us to go to her for Christmas! Not a thought of it! She's totally taken up with this film, all they'll do about Christmas is throw a party right there on the set, and get as high as kites, and then go right back to work. That's the stage they're at, I've seen it all before. No, this is something that only happens once. That's why I didn't just say no. I *couldn't*! I mean, with only one lifetime, and money not all that easy to come by... Well, what would *you* have said?' she challenged warmly.

'How do I know, until I know what you're talking about? What *does* she want us to do?'

'She wants us,' said Tossa, her voice growing faint with mingled wonder and disbelief, 'to take a little girl to India.'

Dominic sat down abruptly on the suitcase and the stubborn lock, as if electing itself a sign and portent for the occasion, clicked smugly into place, ready for off. Though it wasn't as simple as that; for India, at this time of year, you'd want ... what? Not the winter casuals of workaday Oxford, at any rate. Cottons? Light sweaters? Good lord, what was happening? He was taking it seriously, and it could only be some sort of mistake, or somebody's idea of an elaborate joke. He sat staring at her warily, and pushed resolutely out of his mind visions of temples and royal palms, and the legendary beach at Kovalam, and...

'You did say "India"? And you're sure that's what *she* said?'

'I asked her again. She said it twice. She said "Delhi", too. There isn't any mistake.'

'And *both* of us can go?'

'She said so. I said I'd be scared alone.' That was a useful formula, and he knew it; what it meant was: 'Not without Dominic!' and he was duly grateful for it. There were many things of which Tossa was wary and suspicious, after her experiences with parents and step-parents, but very few of which she was scared.

'All expenses paid?' That was how it had sounded.

'Money's no object.'

'But *whose* money?' The only little girl Chloe had was sitting there on the edge of the bed, staring at him with eyes so wide in wonder that the highlights in them soared into silvery domes like the Taj Mahal. And in any case Chloe spent her money as fast as she earned it, not to mention making formidable inroads into her husband's as well.

'Dorette Lester's. It's her little girl we're supposed to escort to Delhi.'

'Who's Dorette Lester?' demanded Dominic, unaware of his blasphemy. Only Julie Andrews shed more sweetness and light, but then, the few films he did see never seemed to be that kind of film.

'She's the American star they brought over to play Marianne in this film Chloe's making. I told you. Everybody thought they'd fight like tigresses, and they fell into each other's arms on first sight, and have been as thick as thieves ever since. That's how it comes that Chloe's willing to lend me to help out Dorette over the kid. She wants us to drive down to Bath and hear all about it, and get fixed up about dates and everything. I suppose we could do that much, anyhow, couldn't we?'

'Today? Now?'

She nodded. The scintillation of desire, fever-white, was still in her eyes. You don't get offered India on a salver every day. 'We can still say no, if we want to.' But she didn't want to, and neither did he. Not if this was on the level. They eyed each other thoughtfully, still chary of believing in such luck.

'There has to be a catch in it,' said Dominic firmly.

She didn't argue; she knew her mother even better than he did, and it was a reasonable assumption that they would trip over a string or two sooner or later. 'It would have to be a big one to tip the scale much, wouldn't it?' she said honestly.

Dominic got up and hoisted the suitcase on which he had been sitting. The coy lock held, ready for any journey. 'You'd better call her back, hadn't you,' he said, rather as if it had been his idea all along, 'and tell her we're coming.'

Some youthful genius from down in the boutique belt, who hatched outrageous ideas on the side and sold them in much the same way as he did outrageous clothes, had come up with the improbable inspiration of making a big musical out of *Sense and Sensibility*, and with his usual luck had found suckers all round him ready to buy the notion that Jane was with it. He had besides – and it was his chief asset

10

– a gift for concocting elegantly dry, agreeable and piquant music, so witty that it turned the most banal lyrics into epigrams, and it was an even bet that the film he had conned his less well-read contemporaries into making would turn out to be not merely a box-office bonanza, but also a surprisingly good film. They had gone the whole hog on casting it. Most of the money in the venture was American, and the producers had insisted on getting Dorette Lester to play Marianne, the 'sensibility' half of the two sisters. The English director, with equal certainty, had declared that no one but Chloe Bliss would do for Eleanor. Chloe's daughter might have cocked a quizzical eyebrow at the idea of her mother standing for 'sense', but it was what she could suggest before the cameras that mattered, not what she really was, and before the cameras or an audience there was nothing Chloe could not be, from an electrifying Ariel in *The Tempest* to an awe-inspiring grande dame in Wilde. Musicals were something new for her, but she took to the form like a duck to water. She sang the outrageously clever songs of the boy genius, half-pop, half-avant-garde, with such conviction that even the composer was startled. He had never taken them all that seriously himself. What he did was juggle the notes and words around a little, and the money came rolling in. He had never ceased to find it funny, but was a little unnerved when he found it could also be moving.

One of those ladies hired to play the youthful Dashwood sisters was turned forty, and the other was thirty-six, and there were plenty of genuine teen-age actresses to be found, what with half the pop singers taking to the boards or the screen or both as to the manner born; yet nobody seemed to find the casting at all strange. Only a year ago Chloe Bliss had added a superlative Peter Pan to her repertoire. And as for Dorette Lester, one of her most passionate admirers had once said that she couldn't sing, couldn't dance, couldn't really do very much in the acting line, and didn't have to; just looking at her was enough. But if she had to act, it had better be in some such part as the hypersensitive and emo-

11

tional Marianne Dashwood, where over-acting, controlled by an intelligent director, wouldn't show.

Dorette had been married in her early twenties, before she became a star. Tossa told Dominic all about it, or as much as she herself had gleaned from Chloe's thumbnail sketch, on the way down to Somerset in the Mini.

'The way I see it, she can't have been much then, and apparently he was rich, and must have been no end of a catch. A couple of years later, and she probably wouldn't have looked at him. He was a graduate from the University of the Punjab, doing post-graduate work in research physics and chemistry over in the States. Anyhow, she married him. And they had this little girl. And then things clicked into place, the way they do at the wrong moment, and she made a hit and grew into a star. And I suppose she got very busy and involved with her job, and he was just as busy with his, and maybe they were too far apart ever to make a go of it. Anyhow, they didn't. She divorced him years ago, and gave herself wholly to her career. And he went back to India, and presumably devoted himself to his.'

'And the little girl,' said Dominic, after a pause for reflection, and in a tone of some wonder, 'is now about to be shipped off after him?'

'That's the way it looks.' And she added doubtfully: 'Maybe just for a visit?' Dominic said nothing to that; he didn't think so, either. 'Well, it seems she's getting married again. Dorette, I mean. Maybe he doesn't react too well to the idea of a ready-made daughter nearly fourteen years old.'

'Or maybe she thinks he won't. I don't suppose she's ever asked him. Or asked the kid what *she* thinks about it.' A possible catch was beginning to appear, and he couldn't help wondering what they were getting themselves into. Still, if the case was as he was beginning to suppose, it could be argued that the little girl would be better off with her father. Or hadn't he wanted her, either? He seemed to have let her go without too much of a fight, and put the width of the world between them.

12

'Still,' said Tossa, mind-reading beside him, 'we shall have to go on and take a look at the whole set-up now, I've committed us to that. We can always back out if we don't like the look of it.'

She looked at Dominic warily along her shoulder; there was something in the acute care he was suddenly giving to his driving, and the look of almost painful detachment on his face, that told her he had found himself abruptly reminded how delicate might be the ground on which they were treading. For Tossa also was the child of an egocentric actress, and her early years also had been bedevilled by her mother's remarriages and haunted by her mother's wit, charm and success, which left her seedling only shady ground in which to grow. He needn't have worried, Tossa was very well able, by this time, to make good her right to a place in the sun. The amiable conflict between mother and daughter was fought on equal terms these days, and as long as Dominic was on her side Tossa had the secure feeling that she was winning. Still, all experience remains there in the memory to be drawn upon at need.

'When you come to think of it,' said Tossa practically, 'I might be just the right person for this job. If the kid is going to be flown off to her father in any case, it might as well be with somebody who's been in much the same boat, and knows the language.' And somebody else, she thought, but did not say, who's never had parent trouble in his life, and doesn't know how lucky he is, but manages to rub off some of the luck on to other people even without realising it.

'It might, at that,' agreed Dominic, cheered. 'Anyhow, let's go and see.'

By which time they were close to the turn that led to the Somerset studio, and the issue was as good as decided.

The Misses Eleanor and Marianne Dashwood sat side by side on a flimsy, gilded, Empire sofa like twin empresses receiving homage, pretty as new paint and something more than content with each other. 'Thick as thieves,' Tossa had

13

said, but in this white, gold and pale blue elegance it seemed an inadmissibly crude phrase – even though the white and gold was gimcrack when you came close to it, and stopped abruptly twenty feet away, to give place to the hollow, cluttered chaos of any other sound stage, littered with skeleton fragments of booms and wiring and cameras and lighting equipment, and a miscellaneous assortment of frayed, bearded, distrait people carrying improbable things and using improbable words in several languages. 'Cheek by jowl' suggested itself, Dominic thought, in some underhand way, but could hardly be entertained in face of Eleanor's resolute and shapely little chin and Marianne's damask-rose cheek. In view of the late-Empire ball gowns of Indian muslin, the daintily deployed curls, dark brown and scintillating gold, and the white silk mittens that stopped only just short of the creamy shoulders, better settle for hand-in-glove. As sure as fate, that was what they were; and anyone around here who had plans that involved manipulating these two Dresden deities had better watch out, because he would be playing a formidable team.

It was an earnest of their sheer professionalism that even between takes they continued to look in character, Chloe gently grave and cool and exceedingly well-bred, Dorette sparkling and distressed by turns, as extrovert as a fountain. Neither of them put her feet up or lit a cigarette. They sat with one foot delicately tucked behind the other, to show a glimpse of a pretty ankle, as young ladies were taught to sit once, long before the miniskirt and the glorious freedom of tights. Dominic revised a half-conceived notion of what Dorette must be like; she might not be a gifted actress, but she was an intelligent diplomat who could make what gifts she had do just as well.

And talk! She could talk the hind leg off a donkey!

'... and then, you see, Tossa — Oh, forgive me! May I call you Tossa? You see, I feel I know you already, your mother has talked so much about you. And you're so *like* her, did you know that?' Tossa knew it, and could hardly fail to be flattered by it, even though she often

14

looked in the glass to find the homely, reassuring outlines of her father's face, less obviously but just as surely there behind the delicate flesh, and the straight, bright, luminous gleam of fun in the eyes that could only have come from him. '... and then, his family made it quite impossible, you know. Oh, Satyavan was simply the new India in person, travelled, educated, sophisticated, brilliant and already rich in his own right ... he had a company making beautiful cosmetics, and another one running travel agencies all over the east and the Middle East. The family were rupee millionaires even before him, but that was all in textiles, cottons and silks, and they really looked down on anything else. An old family, too, and these Punjabis are very proud. So *I* was the undesirable one, you see. His mother was broken-hearted when he married me. She'd been widowed for two years then, and Satyavan was the only child, and of course, you know, *sons* ... *Hindu* sons... Sometimes I think that if only Anjli had been a boy... But she wasn't, and then there weren't any more children.' She wiped away, discreetly and with great dignity, a non-existent tear. 'Really we never had a chance to bridge the gulf. And it *is* a *real* gulf, one would need a lot of patience, and love, and craft ... and luck! And luck we didn't have.'

Dominic hedged his bet still more cautiously. Only a very clever woman would have used the word 'craft' just there. Moreover, Chloe, delicately fanning, her wide eyes on her fictional sister with all the critical admiration of a second watching his expert principal in a duel (and without any qualms whatsoever about the outcome), had raised one eyebrow with a connoisseur's approbation, and the corners of her very charming and very knowing mouth had curled into an infinitesimal and brief smile of pleasure. What chance had any husband with women like these?

'And he didn't even try to get custody of Anjli?' Tossa had seen the omens, too, and reacted with a blunt and discordant question; simply, thought Dominic, to see what would happen.

Dorette's damask cheek bloomed into the most delicious

15

peach colour, and again faded to the waxen white perfection of magnolias. Dominic was fascinated. The magicians of the world would go grey overnight, worrying how she did that in full view of her audience, at a range of a few feet, and in harsh film lighting.

'Tossa, you must be charitable, you must understand... Poor Satyavan, you mustn't think he didn't love her...' (Or why, thought Dominic ruthlessly, would you be shoving her off on to him now, you being the loving mother you are?) 'Yes, he did try ... indeed he tried very hard. But you see, at that time we were so bitter, both of us. And I fought just as hard. Perhaps it was simply that I was American ... for after all, there is an understanding, don't you think so? ... of one's own people? They gave her to me. That was all that mattered then. I didn't think of him ... of his mother ... To an Indian woman sons and grandsons are everything, but even a granddaughter would be such joy ... But it's only afterwards that one realises the cost to other people. You mustn't think I haven't thought about this for a long time, and gone through agony. All these years, ever since she was six years old. I've had the joy of her, and he ... My poor Satyavan...' She made a little poem out of the name this time, the first 'a' muted to a throw-away sound almost like 'u', the second a long sigh of 'aaah'! Her wisp of an embroidered Jane Austen handkerchief came into brief, subdued play. No doubt about it, Dorette was an artist.

Tossa's dry little, gruff little voice said: 'Yes, I do see, he must have missed her terribly!' But Chloe's undisturbed smile said serenely that Dorette was doing very well, and could afford to hold her fire. Perhaps she even read her daughter's implacable motives; whatever the doubts about Dorette's brain, now rapidly being revised, there had never been any doubts about Chloe's. Dominic held his peace, and saw the Taj Mahal clear as in a vision.

'Tossa, there's a time even to give up what one wants and needs, a time to remember ... not other people's wants and needs, but *theirs*. The children's.' Dorette turned her head

16

and gave them the benefit of her full blue stare, radiant and dazzling; and her beauty, of which they had heard so much and thought so little, was absurd, agonising, irresistible. They understood her power, and being immune to it made no difference when the rest of the world was vulnerable. She looked eighteen, agitated, appealing, Marianne to the life. The Austen irony was missing, perhaps, but this was between takes. 'She has a whole family there, wanting and longing for an heir. She has a *kingdom*, you might say. What right have I to keep her from it? What can I give her to make up for it? In America she is just one little girl, not nearly a princess. And my husband...' She looked momentarily doubtful about that word, but shouldered it and went on: 'He has rights, too. She knows nothing of the world *he* can offer her, and she has a right to know everything before she makes a choice. When I marry again...' Oh, noble, that brave lift of her head, facing the whole world's censure for love! Or money. Or *something*! '...she will be watching us from a cool distance, I know that. She knows who her father was, she knows he is far away, and almost lost to her. I want to be honest with her! I want her to go to her father!'

A pale person in an unravelling pullover and a green eyeshade leaned through the pump-room palms and called: 'Any time, Dorrie!' and Miss Lester, switching from emotion and sincerity to a note of sharp practicality which Tossa found almost insulting, called back in quite a different tone: 'Coming, Lennie! Give us three minutes more!' and as promptly returned to character. As though Chloe's two student stand-ins for a New England governess who declined to cross the world had been a couple of cameras trained on her. No more sales-talk was necessary, Chloe's brief, reassuring glance had told her they were sold already; still, for her reputation's sake she kept up the performance in a modified form and at an accelerated tempo.

'My husband is expecting his daughter. I wrote to him a month ago, before I left the States, to tell him that she would be coming. He will be so happy to see her, and so grateful to you.'

For one brief and uncharacteristic moment she looked back, remembering a thin, fastidious face set in the tension of distaste and disbelief as he argued his case in court, with the dignity he was incapable of laying aside, and which had passed for arrogance and coldness. He could hardly be expected to compete with such an artist in heartbreak and tears and maternal desperation as Dorette Lester; sometimes she wondered why he had even tried. And sometimes, too, she wondered exactly why he had waived his rights of access, resigned from his science chair, and left for India immediately after the divorce suit ended. Was it outraged love and implacable anger against the wife who had shucked him off – a broken heart, in fact? Or had he merely extricated himself in shock and disgust from a world he had suddenly realised was not for him, a jungle not denser than, but different from, his own? She knew better than to simplify his withdrawal; herself uncomplicated though occasionally devious, she was subtle enough to recognise a greater subtlety.

'I will give you his address in Delhi, and his mother's, too – Mrs Purnima Kumar – just in case of any contretemps. There will be no difficulty, you'll see. And of course, *all* expenses will be my concern, I'll see that you have plenty of funds. No need even to hurry back, after all, you must see something of India while you're there. Satyavan will be glad to help you make the best use of your time, I know.'

She didn't know anything of the kind, she hadn't been in touch with her ex-husband since he left America, but the family eminence ensured that they would have to put on a show for the visitors; she had learned that much about the Kumars.

'When,' asked Tossa, with careful, measured quietness, 'is Anjli expected to arrive in London?'

'The day after tomorrow. If you could come with me to meet her at London Airport, we could have a night all together, and I could arrange your flight for the next day.

18

Such luck, I have an old, good friend who is filming over there, quite near to Delhi, and I'll wire him to meet your plane and take care of you. If you need anything – but *anything*! – you can call on Ernest, there's nothing he wouldn't do for me. But the journey itself is just too much for a child alone. And we're so pressed, quite behind schedule, you see it's impossible for *me* . . .'

Yes, quite impossible. Not simply because it would inconvenience her, there was more to it than that. India was an alien world into which she had no wish to venture, and Satyavan Kumar was something more distant than a stranger, because he had once been so close. This much of Dorette at least was genuine, she would almost rather die than confront this part of her past again. That all-American marriage – they said this millionaire of hers was a disarmingly nice and simple person – was her life-line, she daren't let go of it for an instant to look behind her.

'You *will* take my little girl over there for me, won't you?' Knock off the calculated charm, and in its way it was still a cry from the heart.

'Dorette! You ready there?'

'Yes, Lennie! We're right with you! *Tossa, dear . . .*'

'Yes, Miss Lester . . . Yes, of course we'll take her!'

'Darling . . . so grateful . . . my mind at rest now . . . *Sure, Lennie, coming!* Day after tomorrow . . . Heathrow . . . I'll phone you the details . . . what was that Midshire number again?' And Chloe laughed, not aloud, just a faint purring sound of contentment, and hugged and kissed her own daughter briefly.

When they crept out of the sound stage she was singing, without a trace of irony, back there behind them in the furnished corner bright as a nova:

> '*When will you learn to moderate, my love,*
> *The ardour of a heart that can be broken . . .*'

Tossa sat dour and silent in the Mini for some moments after they had made their way out of the lot and turned north for Midshire and Dominic's blessedly normal home. Then she said in a dubious voice: 'Of course, for all we know the father may be no better. But at least he ought to have his chance. And anyhow, *this* one's contracting out, so *somebody* has to do something.' And in a moment, with reviving optimism about the general state of man: 'We'll see what your people say about it.'

All Dominic said was: 'I still don't see where the catch is, but there has to be one somewhere.'

What Dominic's people said, almost in unison though they were tackled separately, was: 'Of course go! You'd be crazy not to. *Always* say yes to opportunity, or it may never offer again.' And his mother, viewing Tossa's grave face with sympathy, added: 'If the worst comes to the worst, *bring her back*. We can fight out the rest of it afterwards.'

So they were all there at Heathrow to meet Anjli's plane, Dorette in mink and cashmere and Chanel perfume, Chloe booted and cased in leather dyed to fabulous shades of purple and iris, with something like a space helmet on her extremely shapely little head and Ariel's formidable and lovely make-up on her clever faun's face, Dominic and Tossa top-dressed for the frost outside, but with their modest cases full of hurriedly assembled cottons and medium-weight woollens, mostly organised out of nowhere by Dominic's mother. Who now had her feet up at home, a drink at her elbow and a paperback in her hand, and only the mildest regrets at facing a quieter Christmas than she had expected. It was a long time since she'd had her husband to herself over the Christmas holidays. And what fools these children would have been to pass up India, upon any consideration, when it fell warm, aromatic and palpitating into their arms.

In the arrivals lounge the privileged crowded to the doors to see their kin erupting through passport control. Dorette swooped ahead in a cloud of pastel mink and subtle fragrance.

'*Darling!* Oh, honey, how *lovely* to see you!'

20

The girl turned an elegant head just in time to present her left cheek to the unavoidable kiss, adjusted her smile brightly and extricated herself more rapidly and dexterously than Dominic would have believed possible.

'Hi, Mommy! How have you been? Gee, what a flight, I'm about dead on my feet. Oh, hi! You must be Miss Bliss, Mommy's told me so much about you, and all about this darling film. My, that outfit's *keen*, you know that? It's just a *dream* . . . !'

If ever the selfconscious and phoney and the real and eager and young met in one voluble utterance, this was the time. But it took somebody Chloe's age to respond to all the nuances at once, and Chloe had relegated herself deliberately to a back seat, and didn't mean to be turfed out of it. Let Tossa, who prided herself so on her maturity, make her own way through the quicksands. Chloe smiled, kissed the pale golden cheek and made a cool neutral murmur in the small, fine, close-set golden ear.

'And here's my daughter Tossa, who's coming with you to Delhi . . . And Dominic Felse, a friend of Tossa's . . . a friend of all of us . . .'

'Why, sure,' said the clear, thrilling little voice, aloof as a bird, 'any friend of yours! I just hope I get in as one of the family, too.' She put a thin, amber hand into Tossa's, smiled briefly and brilliantly, and passed on to Dominic with markedly more interest. 'Hullo, Dominic! Gee, I'm lucky, being so well looked after. I sure appreciate it, I really do.'

So this was the poor little girl! Little she was, in the physical sense, well below average height for a fourteen-year-old, and built of such fine and fragile bones that she contrived to seem smaller than she was. She wore a curly fun-fur coat in a mini-length, and a small round fur cap to match, in dappled shades of tortoiseshell, like a harlequin cat. Her long, slim legs were cased in honeycomb lace tights and flexible red leather boots that stopped just short of her knee, and the honey of her skin glowed golden through the comb. A fur shoulder-bag slung on a red strap

21

completed the outfit. But the accessories of her person were every bit as interesting. Her fingernails were manicured into a slightly exaggerated length, and painted in a pink pearl colour, deeper at the tips. The shape of her lips had been quite artfully and delicately accentuated and their colour deepened to a warm rosy gold. A thick braid of silky black hair hung down to her waist, a red ribbon plaited into it. Half her face was concealed behind the largest butterfly-rimmed dark glasses Dominic had ever seen; but the part of her that showed, cheeks and chin, was smooth and beautifully shaped as an Indian ivory carving, and almost as ageless. Sophistication in one miniature package stared up at Dominic unnervingly through the smoke-grey lenses. The obscurity of this view suddenly irked her. She put up her free hand in a candid gesture of impatience, and plucked off her glasses to take a longer, clearer, more daunting look at him.

The transformation was dazzling. Thin, arched brows, very firm and forthright, came into view, and huge, solemn, liquid dark eyes; and the face was suddenly a child's face as well as a mini-model's, eager, critical and curious; and presently, with hardly a change in one line of it, greedy. No other word for it.

She was at the right age to wish to be in love, and to be able to fall in love almost deliberately, wherever a suitable object offered. Dominic was a suitable object. He saw himself reflected in the unwavering eyes, at once an idol for worship and a prey marked down.

Over Anjli's head he caught Tossa's eye, marvellously meaningful in a wooden face. They understood each other perfectly. No need to look any farther for the catch; they had found it.

II

'I was here, once, said Anjli, unfolding the coloured
brochure of Delhi across her lap with desultory interest. 'In
India, I mean. But I can't remember much about it now,
it's so long ago.'

'Your mother didn't tell us that,' Tossa said. 'Was she
with you?'

'No, only my father. She didn't want to come, she was
filming. It was the year before she divorced him. I was only
just five. I used to know a little Hindi, too, but I've forgotten it all now.'

Her voice was quite matter-of-fact; she felt, as far as
they could detect, no regrets over America, and no qualms
or anticipation at the prospect of India. She had been
brought up largely by competent people paid to do the job,
and she was under no illusions about her own position or
theirs. A child in her situation, intelligent and alert as she
was, would have to acquire a protective shell of cynicism in
order to survive, thought Tossa. Anjli knew that there was
money on both sides of her family, and that however she
might be pushed around from one parent to the other, that
money would have to maintain her in the style to which she
was accustomed. As for the cool equanimity with which she
had parted from her mother at London Airport, who could
be surprised by it, when she had spent most of her young
life as isolated from her mother as from her distant and
forgotten father?

'He brought me to see his mother, I think, but I don't
remember her at all. I guess she must have been pretty
upset at his marrying in America, like that, and staying
away all that time. They're very clannish, aren't they?'

'Very much like the rest of us, I expect,' said Tossa.
'She'll be pleased enough when she has you on a more per-

manent basis, I bet.'

The Indian Airlines plane hummed steadily towards Delhi, half its passengers dozing, like Dominic in the seat across the gangway from them. Strange, thought Anjli, without resentment, almost with appreciation, how neatly Tossa had steered him into that place, though Anjli had designed that he should sit beside her, as on the long flight over. This small reverse she could afford to take in her stride; she had time enough, she calculated optimistically, to detach him from his Tossa before they left Delhi again. As yet they were only one hour inland from Bombay. The adventure had hardly begun.

'Oh, I haven't made up my mind yet about staying,' she said firmly. 'I don't know whether I'm going to like it here. It's kind of a corny country, don't you think?' She frowned down at the coloured pictures of the Red Fort and the Qutb Minar. 'All this old stuff, I mean, what's the *point*? In the States we've got everything *new*, and after all, I've grown up there. This will be an experience, but I don't figure I'm going to want to stay here too long.'

She was quite firm about it; and on reflection, Tossa thought, she was quite capable of demanding to be taken back again when India palled, and getting her own way, too. Dorette had made her plans; but so might Anjli, and there was a good deal of Dorette in Anjli, enough to make the struggle a dangerously even one if it ever came to that. And yet . . .

'Do you really think,' said Anjli suddenly, her cheek turned to the window, where the blinding light clung and quivered as it touched her lips, 'she'll be glad to have me? She's old, and she *hated* it when he married Mommy.'

'But you're not Dorette, you're you . . . partly her son. You're her only grandchild. She'll be glad,' said Tossa with certainty.

It was the nearest they had come, in all that long and tedious journey, to asking and giving sympathy; and even now Tossa felt herself to be on thin ice. Very aloof, very independent, this child; she'd be infuriated if you tried to

24

mother her, when she'd managed for so long without any mothering. Not the clinging kind, Anjli; except, of course, in a predatory fashion to Dominic's arm when the slimmest chance offered. Inscrutable, dangerous and to be respected, that was Satyavan Kumar's daughter. Tossa didn't know whether to be sorrier for the grandchild or the grandmother. Somehow, between these two, the face of the father eluded her imagination; for it had never entered Dorette's head to show her a photograph of Satyavan. Probably she hadn't even kept one, once the man himself was out of her life.

Anjli, her cheek against the sun-warmed glass, watched the baked, thirsty land revolve beneath them, presenting a changing, circling pattern of white buildings, radiating roads, scattered green trees dispersed in a rose-red land-scape. The palette of North India, apart from the hills, is a wonderful range of reds and oranges and browns, glittering with drought. In winter the green of foliage looks faded and silvery against it, and the violent crimsons and purples of early flowering trees explode like fireworks.

'Look, Delhi!'

Dominic awoke, and came to lean across them both and peer down with them at the fabled city, older than Alex-ander, eight cities superimposed upon one another, overlap-ping, showing faintly through like a palimpsest. The radi-ant light picked out minarets, domes, pompous white office blocks, the superb sweep of the King's Way, ruled across New Delhi in rose-pink, lined on either side with vivid grass and the embroidered mirror-glitter of water, cluster-ing green of parks, the spinning wheel of Connaught Place with all its radial roads straight as arrows. For some mo-ments they had a perfect sketch-map before them, then the plane settled lower and selected its way in to the inter-national airport, and they were left with a narrowing circle of the south-western cantonment, ruled in rectangular blocks, gathering, solidifying, growing to lifesize.

Anjli, gazing dubiously down at the city of which she was mortally afraid, settled her brow artfully against Dominic's arm and counted, shrewdly, her blessings. Never

25

look too far ahead; now is what matters. Because there isn't any tomorrow, and you can't make much capital out of yesterday, it slips through your fingers; but now is something there'll always be, even if it changes its shape.

Dominic saw the tense line of her mouth and cheek, and didn't move his arm. They watched Delhi come up to meet them, a floating city, red and white, wonderful.

The touch-down was brisk and gentle and indifferently expert. And at Palam Ernest Felder was waiting for them.

He was fifty years old, but looked younger because of his springy step and dapper carriage. They said he had given Dorette her first chance in films, years ago, and stayed a close friend of hers ever since, though by all accounts at one time he would have liked to be more to her than a friend. He had been the minor celebrity then, and she the raw beginner; now she was the reigning star of the old, wholesome school of sweet family entertainment, and he was still a minor celebrity, perhaps a rung or two lower down the ladder than when they had met, but still a director of mild distinction. Or was it co-director this time? Dorette had mentioned an Indian director who was sharing the responsibility with him on this co-production.

He met them as soon as they crossed the apron of sandbrown earth and entered the airport buildings. A large, muscular hand reached for Dominic's, acknowledging the male as automatically in charge. A shaggy, brindled grey head inclined punctiliously, a weathered, philosophical face, lined with humour and self-indulgence, beamed welcome at them all. A very well-kept body, athletic and lean, made the most of a beautifully-cut grey suit.

'Mr Felse? I'm Felder. Dorrie wired me to look out for you. Miss Barber, you're very welcome to India. I hope you're not too tired after the journey?' He turned to Anjli, and contemplated her long and fondly, while she stared back at him unblinkingly and let her small hand lie limply in his. 'And you must be Dorrie's little girl. Well, well, I haven't seen you since you were knee-high to a kitten.'

26

Anjli, on her dignity, looked down her nose and said:
'How do you do, Mr Felder!' in her best party tones. But
he looked kind and easy-going, and his voice recalled
America in this alien land, and she could not help warming
to him. 'It's sure nice to have somebody here who belongs,'
she said, for once without calculation, and her passive
fingers stirred and gripped confidingly.

'Girlie, you're going to have no trouble at all that way,
not while my bunch are here just outside town. Film people
I bet you know, and film people are the same the world
over, even when you've got ten sorts together, the way we
have here. I've got 'em all laid on for you, a real party, so
Delhi's going to feel like home. I've got the boys outside
with the truck, you don't have to do a thing but just hand
over to us, and we do everything.'

'It's really very kind of you,' said Tossa, and meant it,
'but I suppose we ought to contact Mr Kumar as soon as
possible, oughtn't we?'

'So you ought, my dear, so you ought. But it's coming on
evening, and you've all three just been rushed across the
world, and it's my belief you need tonight to unwind and
put your best moods and faces on ready for the moment of
truth.' Bless him, he wasn't going to pretend for a moment
that anything about this was easy or normal. He knew his
Dorette from long since, and had learned to approach the
crises she created with caution and philosophy. 'Now I
know she won't have wired him exactly when to expect you,
or why would she hand things over to me? Yes, I know she
wrote him a warning, three, four weeks ago, but that's the
size of it. I know my girl! That cost her plenty. Now before you go to him you've got to have a roof over your heads
that you don't owe to him, and friends right there behind
you, so you can say simply: "Look, here I am. Am I welcome?" and if not, well, all right, then, that's that, good-
bye. Sorry you've been troubled, and no hard feelings.
We're not beggars, are we, honey? We've got places of our
own to go to, and feet of our own to stand on. Right?'

He was looking at Anjli. There was a bloom of colour

27

flooding the honey of her cheeks, and she looked tall and grave and very independent. 'Right!'

'So I reckon tomorrow morning will be time enough for Mr Kumar. Mornings are the time for starting enterprises. Right?'

'Right! And we can have this evening! We haven't seen *anything* yet. All we did at Bombay was get out of one plane at Santacruz and into another.'

'Miss Lester did say,' agreed Dominic hopefully, 'that she would arrange a hotel for us. We took it for granted that Tossa and I would need one, of course...'

'Don't say another word, it's all taken care of. I've booked you all in at Keen's Hotel. It's south of town, off the Lodi Road, but it's cheaper than most and just as good, and I reckoned you might want to stay around town a while, since you *are* here on Dorrie's errand. Shame to waste that air fare, who knows if it may not be once in a lifetime? How's that? Sound OK?'

'Sounds wonderful!' said Tossa with heartfelt gratitude. You didn't find a thoughtful host of this kind every day. 'It's terribly good of you.'

'Come on, then, and let's pick up your luggage, they should have turfed it out by now.' He took Anjli by the hand as naturally as a tried and trusted uncle, and surprisingly she let him. They might all get a little dizzy and confused later, if Mr Felder kept up this pace and all his unit matched up, but at the moment he was certainly a huge relief.

In through the teeming halls of Palam, as loud and busy and stunning as any other international airport, but peacock-hued with glorious saris and bleached white with invading sunlight; and out to the stands where the luggage was deposited, and the porters waited bright-eyed, heads swathed in red cloths, ready to pounce on whatever cases were claimed. Two of them secured the items Dominic indicated, and hoisted them to their padded heads. Dominic would have lifted one case himself, but Felder nudged him good-humouredly aside.

28

'Don't! It doesn't cost much, even if you over-tip, and these boys have to make a living. This country sure has a lot of people to feed.'

Anjli stood on the steps, and looked at the barren, parched, russet and gold land from which her father had sprung, a waste of reds, dead-rose-petal browns, tawny sand, punctuated with patches of vivid green grass and frail, newly-budding trees. A pallid forecourt, a circle of gardens, a silver-grey road winding away towards the distant white walls of the town. But mostly one level of dust-fine soil, drowned in sunlight so sharp and thin that it seemed there must be frost in the air. In her fine woollen cardigan suit she felt warm enough, and yet there was a clarity that cut like knives when she breathed. And this was Delhi in December.

She didn't remember anything, or at least, not with any part of mind or memory. Only her blood stirred strangely, recapturing some ancestral rapport. Not necessarily in affection; rather with a raising of hackles, aware of compulsions not altogether congenial. It was too bright, too dry, too clear, too open; there was nowhere to hide.

'This way. We're not supposed to park private stuff round here, but what can you do? These foreigners!' Felder led the way briskly round the corner of the buildings to the blinding white concrete where the airport bus was filling up with plump ladies in saris and ponderous gentlemen in white cottons and European overcoats. The truck turned out to be a minibus, from which two unmistakable young Americans leaned to grin at them hospitably and offer large, amiable hands.

'Tom Hoskins is our driver-cum-handyman. There isn't much Tom can't do. And this is Joe Salt, assistant cameramen. We've got it dead easy here, mostly we're playing second-fiddle to the Indians, and believe me, Ganesh Rao knows exactly what he wants, and nine-tenths of the time he's dead right, so ours is a sinecure. Get aboard, ladies, choose your seats, we'll take you round through the city for a ride.'

29

They climbed aboard willingly, eyes round and attentive at the windows, intent on missing nothing.

'Shouldn't we at least check in at the hotel?' asked Dominic.

'So we will, laddie, so we will, on our way out to Mehrauli. Don't want to haul this luggage around, do we? This will be a lightning tour specially for you, because we've got to go right in to the shopping centre at Connaught Circus to pick up one of the gang, and then we're bound due south for the edge of the town, where we're filming. We'll be quite close to Keen's on the way out, and drop your stuff off there. Straight to the town office, Tom, Ashok will be there by now, we're a mite late.'

Tom drove with the verve and aplomb which they were later to associate with Sikh taxi-drivers, and in particular with the devoted virtuosi, also mostly Sikhs and invariably young, who drove the wappish little scooter-rickshaws around the town. Clearly he had been here long enough to know his way around and to have bettered the impetuous elan of the native motorists. They clung to their seats (though Anjli tended rather to cling to Dominic) and stared their fill; and Mr Felder, with wide shoulders braced easily against the panelling and long legs stretched across the gangway, commented spasmodically on the unfolding scene of Delhi.

On either side the steel-grey road the overwhelming brownness of North India, at first a monotone, dissolved, as they penetrated it, into a marvellous spectrum of shades and textures, which yet were all brown. Even the grass was brown, a dry, subtle shade with tints of green breathing through it, to indicate that against first appearances it still lived. Beyond all question the air was alive, the light was alive, the incredibly brilliant sky was alive, radiantly blue and flecked with a few sailing feathers of cloud to emphasize its depth of colour. At first they drove across the barren brown earth as over a dead calm sea, the steely road now growing russet with the reflected glow, its dusty fringes lined with curious crude baskets of rust-coloured

30

iron, like fireless braziers. 'Newly-planted trees,' said Felder, forestalling the question; and then they could glimpse the tender green saplings just peering over their bars. 'You'll see 'em all over the new suburbs. They won't always be eyesores.' Then they were among scattered small houses, dropped almost accidentally about the dun-coloured plain, and abruptly the white buildings congealed into a residential road. On their left rose the heaving brown flank of the Ridge, on their right, from clustering trees, soared a phantasmagoria of imposing buildings of every possible design and style, regularly spaced like huge summer-houses in a giant's garden. 'The Diplomatic Enclave. They suggested every country should build its embassy in its own national style. See those dark-blue domes? Pakistan did that! You ought to walk through, some time, you won't believe your eyes. And that huge palace beyond, that's the Ashoka Hotel. Prestige job. You won't believe that, either . . .'

From Willingdon Crescent they caught glimpses of the dome of Rashtrapati Bhavan and the twin blocks of the government secretariat, a brief rear view of the spacious buildings of the new city; then they were careering up Irwin Road, head over ears into the pandemonium of modern Delhi's street life at last, between banks and restaurants and cinemas plastered with posters tall as towers and vivid as the rainbow, caught in a whirling current of cars, buses, bicycles, pedestrians and motorbikes and scooters towing canopied rickshaws, extravagantly painted with flowers, birds and garlands, like some wonderful hybrid between an old-fashioned hansom cab and the cabin of a canal-boat. This brilliant river brought them suddenly to the whirlpool of New Delhi's shopping centre, the wheel of radiating streets they had seen from the air.

'Drive round Connaught Place, Tom, just once, let them have a look at the nearest thing we've got to Piccadilly.'

It was much more spacious than Piccadilly, a large, regular circle of park in the centre, ringed with a broad road and a colonnade of white shops, and eight radial roads lancing away from the centre like the spokes of a wheel.

31

Tom made the circuit of it at speed, for here there was less traffic and more space, and the pedestrians had withdrawn to the raised sidewalk that was sheltered by the colonnade.

'The outer ring is where we're going ... Connaught Circus. If you ever want to shop, you could do worse than start here. OK, Tom, make for the office.'

Tom took the nearest radial road, and turned left into Connaught Circus, the rim of the wheel. Banks, garages, restaurants, shops flickered past them in procession, then intervals of trees and grass, and curious quiet islands of older buildings cheek by jowl with the new. They halted before a low green hedge, a narrow strip of garden, and a tall, plain, Victorian colonial house.

'Temporary headquarters. Down south, near Mehrauli, we've got a couple of villas for living quarters, but we shall only be there a few days, then we're headed for Benares to do the Deer Park scenes at Sarnath, right where they happened. But this is where we keep our gear and do the office work.'

'What is the film you're making?' Tossa asked curiously.

'Didn't Dorrie tell you? It's an epic about the life of the Buddha. Time was when it would have been called: *World, Farewell!* or some such title. Nowadays we do these things straight, and simply call it *The Buddha*. After all, if you can have a film called *The Bible* you can have one called *The Buddha*, can't you? That's what the producer wants. But Ganesh Rao says the accent is on the man, and it ought really to be called *Siddhartha*. So my guess is, that's what it'll be called in the end.'

'I've *heard* of the Buddha,' Anjli said delicately, not committing herself to total ignorance, 'but I don't really know the story. Could you tell it to me?'

'Ashok is the man you want, he'll tell you everything you need to know. Give him a blast, Tom, he can't have heard us come.'

Tom obliged. The fan-lighted door of the house opened promptly, and a small, slender man in close-fitting trousers and a grey achkan came dancing down the steps with a

32

music-case tucked under his arm. His eyes were black and long-lashed, his smile aloof and courteous, and his colour palest bronze. Surprisingly the rest of his features, full, mobile lips, hooked nose and jutting cheek-bones, were so jagged that he looked like a head by Epstein, and a good one, at that.

He said: 'Welcome to Delhi!' in a soft, shy voice, and clambered nimbly into the minibus, where he dumped his music-case between his feet and clasped fine, broad-jointed hands across his stomach. The first two fingers of his left hand were scored at the tips with deep, stained grooves, many-times-healed and many-times-re-opened wounds, smeared with cream that glistened when the light caught it.

'Meet Ashok Kabir,' said Felder, 'our musical director. You ask him nicely, Anjli, and he'll play you some of his music for *Siddhartha* presently, when we get him warmed up. Ashok, the little lady wants you to tell her all about this film of ours.'

Anjli Kumar and Ashok Kabir looked at each other suddenly, attentively, at a range of about one foot, and in their own personal ways fell in love at first sight. Dominic, watching with sharpened senses, thought, good lord, I never dreamed it would be that easy. I needn't have worried, I was just standing in for whoever it was going to be. Anjli saw the native, the initiate, the authority, whose grace was such that he was willing to share what he knew with whoever went to meet him in the right spirit. Ashok, the artist, and himself complete, saw the homing exile unaware of her wishes or her needs, a fragmented child unable to recognise her fractures, much less repair them. They looked at each other with wonder, interest and respect, and had nothing yet to say.

'Now down Janpath, fast as you like,' said Felder contentedly, 'but take it easy where it crosses Rajpath – did I tell you that's the King's Way, you folks? Janpath is the Queen's Way! – so they can get a look right along to the government buildings. You think you've seen something when you've seen the Mall, in London? Wait till you get a load of this! And then go round the back of the Lodi Park to Keen's, and we'll drop the bags off and sign in ...'

Keen's was an old-fashioned but English-run hotel, in an ancient white Indian house that turned a blank face to the street on all sides, and lived a full life about its internal courtyard and gardens, with a balcony for every room – every suite, if the truth be told – on its first and second floors, where the guests were housed. There was but one way in, masked by a tall green hedge; and inside, there was peace and almost silence, all street noises excluded. Room-boys dressed as rajas made off with the baggage, but they turned out to be one of the trimmings of every hotel, even the most modest, and were amiable enough at very low cost. The new arrivals lingered only long enough to stop feeling stunned, and to extract from their bags the coats which Felder insisted they would need in an hour or so. Then they were borne away to the two villas near Hauz Khas, on the most southerly fringe of the city, where a couple of trucks and a large saloon car had just unloaded the exhausted company from Mehrauli.

The din of voices was deafening but reassuring; who could feel inhibited or a stranger where the general babel made it possible to talk nonsense and not be brought to answer for it? And the array of faces, several of them still in make-up, baffled memory and withdrew names, making it necessary, after a while, to enquire discreetly about the dominant members of the collective; but that was taken for granted, and everyone answered cheerfully for himself. In a large, charming, rather bare room, with tall windows looking out on a neglected garden, they circulated and ate and drank, and in an unexpected fashion were at home. The girls – there seemed to be several girls – kept disappearing, and coming back with something freshly cooked. Everything was improvised, but everything worked. It might not be Indian – how could they judge? – but it was calming and reassuring and just what they needed.

34

Ashok Kabir sat cross-legged on a cushion, and cradled his sitar in his arms, its long, beautiful, polished body reclined upon his shoulder, the twenty moveable frets gleaming and quivering like nerves along its slender teak neck, the larger sounding gourd at the base of the throat nuzzling his heart. Six main strings, so they said, and nineteen sympathetic ones! And those strings were the reason why the fingers with which he controlled them were gashed deep, and never could be healed. And we think western music is a hard apprenticeship!

'...so Prince Siddhartha was born to the King Suddhodana and his Queen Maya,' said Ashok in his soft voice, 'and all the auguries were auspicious, though a little puzzling. The wise men told the king that his son would certainly be a very great leader, there was only some doubt as to *what kind*. They said that if ever the prince was allowed to set eyes on an old man, a sick man, a dead man and a holy monk, then he would be the lord of a very great kingdom, but not of this world. And as the king preferred that his son should go on ruling after him in the normal and profitable way of this world, he took good care to bring up Siddhartha in a kind of benevolent imprisonment, surrounded by every kind of pleasant diversion, and excluded from him all sickness and ugliness and pain. And when he grew up they married him successfully to the most beautiful of all the noblewomen of the land...'

'Thank you, darling!' said Kamala sweetly, and bowed her acknowledgements with hands prayerfully pressed together and head inclined. She wore a white silk sari embroidered with green and silver thread, and looked rather like the Indian Miss World, only more so. She was, according to Felder, as clever as she was beautiful, and nearly as acquisitive, and it had cost plenty to get her to play the heroine.

'...the sweet Yashodhara ... with whom in any case he was already in love, and she with him...'

'Naturally!' murmured Kamala, with a glance at the statuesque figure and consciously splendid countenance of

35

her lord Siddhartha, holding court on the other side of the room with a fresh lime soda in one hand. 'Who could help it?'

They had seen that face on one of the outsize posters in Janpath or Irwin Road, early that evening. There was no mistaking it. Felder had translated the lettering of the name for them; Barindra Mitra, one of the popular demi-gods, for top-flight film stars in India are little less than deities. Barindra Mitra sat cross-legged on his couch as on a throne, all the more devastating in majesty because he was still in costume, swathed in short gold tunic and white silk robe, with one bronze shoulder naked, and on his head a tower-like crown studded with property jewels.

'But the prince grew restive with being cooped up, and soon outgrew all his pleasure-gardens and palaces, and would go out into the city of Kapilavastu. And when he couldn't dissuade him, the king sent out orders through the city that everyone who was sick or ugly or maimed or old should be kept out of the way for the occasion. All the same, when the prince drove through the town with his faithful charioteer Channa, he was suddenly confronted by something he had never seen before in his life, and had never realised existed ... an aged, senile decrepit, miserable relic of a man at the end of his span. Old Age in person!'

'At your service!' said the jaunty young man who was just handing round a tray of savoury patties. His arms and legs still bore the traces of the old man's artful make-up, and he was still draped in picturesque rags, but he had shed the wig and beard, huddled shaggily at this moment in a corner of the long couch like a sleeping Yorkshire terrier, and his face, but for two painted patches of grained grey-ness on the cheeks, was in its smooth, high-coloured prime.

'Naturally he asked whatever this creature could be, and if it was really a man at all, and whether it had been born so, or this was a visitation from the gods. And Channa had to tell him at last that what he saw was the common lot of all men at the end, that this poor wreck had once been as young and ardent as the prince himself, and that some day the prince himself would be as was this old man. And Siddhartha drove back to the palace terribly shaken. And that's the scene they've been shooting in Mehrauli this afternoon.'

'Mehrauli being only a village, properly speaking,' said the director Ganesh Rao, in his immaculate and unaccented English, 'but perhaps nearer to Kapilavastu than anything one could fake up in the city. And if you want an excitable but manageable crowd laid on in moments, it's just the place.'

So that was why three of them were still so fresh from the cameras that they had not got rid of make-up and costumes yet. Old Age, Channa the charioteer, and Prince Siddhartha : Govind Das and Subhash Ghose, two professional Bengali character actors, and Barindra Mitra, the star. Anjli sat cross-legged on a cushion on the floor, squarely facing Ashok, and copying his pose to the last finger-curve of the relaxed hand that lay in his lap, the hand with the plectrum strapped to the index finger. She took her dark, disconcerting gaze from his face long enough to look round them all, and enjoy the attention she was getting as Dorette Lester's little girl. Felder had been right, the film world is one the world over.

'Tomorrow,' said Ganesh Rao, digging thick, strong fingers into his thatch of black hair, 'we're going to finish the other two scenes there, the encounters with disease and death.'

'So he did go again,' Anjli said, and her grave eyes came back to Ashok's face.

'Twice, and he saw what really happens to men. And in the meantime Yashodhara had a son, but it was too late to deflect her husband, however much he loved them both. He saw that age and sickness and death were waiting for them, as well as for him, and that nobody had ever found a way of triumphing over these evils. So he named the child Rahula ... that means a fetter, because the child bound him like a chain. And the prince rode out one more time, and he met an ascetic monk, who had forsaken the world for solitude, in search of the ultimate peace that no one knows. And after this Siddhartha brooded on the need to find this transcendent peace, this freedom from the wheel of recurring sufferings, not only for himself, not first for himself, but for his dearest, and after them for all men. And one night after the pleasures and entertainments of the palace were over, and all the court lay asleep, he got up in the small hours and looked at his sleeping wife and son, and went out from them silently in search of the way. The king had every gate guarded, being afraid of this, but all the guards slept, and all the gates opened of themselves to let Siddhartha go free.'

'Play some of the music,' suggested Kamala, leaning over him from behind in a drift of pale silk and perfume. 'Play my song, and then the theme of the departing, let Anjli hear how you can make a folk melody and a classical meditation out of the same notes. Do you know what is a raga, Anjli? They are the basic material for all our classical music, and there are thousands of them, the ragas, each for a special time and season, and a special mood, so that in a few rising and descending notes you have the mind's first statement, the one thought out of which a work of art grows. Tell them, Ashok!'

Ashok explained with his fingers. The teak neck of the sitar leaned confidingly into his shoulder, his scarred fingers pressed the main strings, and with the plectrum he picked out a brief, rising phrase, and brought it sighing down again to dissolve where it had begun. A handful of notes tossed into the air and caught again. He repeated it slowly, to let them follow the sound, and then took it up in tentative chords and began to embroider. Not yet the form in which they had occasionally heard classical ragas, but turning the notes into a simple, folk melody, something even the western ear could accept readily and even memorise. Kamala took up the thread and began to sing wordlessly, in a sweet, forward, wailing voice, the gentle caterwauling of a deserted kitten.

38

'But that's something even we would find approachable,' said Tossa, astonished. 'I expected it to be much more difficult.'

'It's meant to be approachable, it must reach everybody in this form. If I do not hear it sung in the streets, once the film is shown, I shall be disappointed. And for that it must be grasped on the wing, it will be heard only once. It is the lullaby Yashodhara sings to Rahula after she discovers that her lord is gone. And this is how it will be heard at his going.'

This time the theme budded slowly, and began to uncurl in a meditative development. The plangent string tone of the sitar, no longer unfamiliar even in the West, swelled until from a curiously intimate and secret solo instrument it had become a full orchestra. Its sweetness and strangeness had a hypnotic effect, to which the nerves responded, and even though the expected acceleration did not come, or only in a strictly modified form, the usual mounting tension and excitement was present no less, drawing mind and senses taut in almost painful concentration. Some music lulls; this disturbed. And so it should, for it expressed the renunciation of the world and the assumption of the world's burden in one symbolic act. They could almost see the solitary figure steal silently through the apartments of the palace, leaving the sleepers sleeping, and the gates one by one opening before him, until he bestowed his ornaments upon Channa, exchanged his rich garments for the plain yellow robe of a huntsman in the forest, cut off the princely knot of his hair, sent back in sorrow his charioteer and his white horse Kantaka, and walked forward alone into the darkness to do battle with life and death. And at the moment when he vanished the music died away in a shuddering sigh and broke off, unfinished.

Everyone stirred and drew breath, otherwise the silence lasted for a moment; then Anjli asked:

'Do the ragas all have names?'

'Yes, they have names. This is Raga Aheer Bhairab. It is a morning raga.'

'And it has a special purpose? A special mood, Kamala said?'

'It is to be played,' said Ashok, stroking his still faintly vibrating strings, 'in the early hours of the morning, when the guests are departing.'

Felder drove them back to Keen's Hotel about nine o'clock in the evening, a little dazed, a little silent. Anjli was clutching the copy of *The Life of the Buddha* which Ashok had lent her. And again Felder had been quite right, they needed their coats; the air was sharp and very cold, the sky above crackling with stars.

'Where is this place you've got to go? Rabindar Nagar? That's one of the newish suburbs that are spreading out westwards, isn't it? Will you find your way all right?'

'I've got a town plan,' said Dominic. 'We'll find it.'

'I'd come with you, but we want to finish the Mehrauli shots tomorrow, and if we make it we're off by air to Benares the next morning to do the Deer Park scenes. I don't suppose you'll have any trouble. But just in case you do need any help, give me a ring in the evening. You've got the villa number and the office, I'll be one end or the other. Give me a ring anyhow. I'll be glad to know how you get on.'

'We'll do that. And thanks for everything.'

III

Rabindar Nagar was close to the western fringe of the town, completely cut off from any view of New Delhi itself by the long, undulating brown hump of the Ridge. It was a suburb as yet only half-built, every house in it an individual undertaking and of individual and often surprising taste. This was not where the very rich would build, or the very fashionable; but there was plenty of money here, too, putting up those fanciful white villas and running those substantial cars. Here came the wealthy retired tradesman, the Sikh taxi proprietor who had plenty of transport at his disposal, and didn't mind the long run from town, the small factory owner who couldn't rise to a property in the tree-shaded, fashionable enclaves of the city itself, and the young artist of independent means who preferred detachment, possibly from the distractions of traffic and noise, probably from too autocratic parents. Whimsy could have its fling on a small and fairly economical scale here, and on a limited site. The houses sat cheek by jowl along the neat roadways, and between their rear compounds ran narrow lanes by which the hawkers and salesman reached the kitchen doors. The rusty iron baskets that shielded new trees bristled everywhere along the roadsides. The sounds, in the early morning, were a curious mixture of domestic and wild, of cars starting up, of the wavering trade calls of the ironing man and the fresh vegetable man along the rear courtyards, bidding for custom, and distant and eerie from the west the wail of jackals prowling the harsh brown land. The ironing man's little cart, with its small charcoal brazier at one end, halted under back windows; women came bustling out with armfuls of laundry to be ironed, and the hot smell of the smoothed cotton and linen was as savoury on the air as bread. Schoolgirls came demurely out of front compound gates in their uniform shalwar and kameez, close-waisted tunic and wide trousers neatly fitted at the ankles, gauze scarf draped over the shoulders with ends floating behind. The bane of all tomboys, those scarves, the first thing to get discarded when they ran out to play hockey on the open patch of ground after school.

Part of this open space was occupied, at the moment, by a cluster of brown tents, in which lived Orissan building workers, employed on two half-finished houses just along the main road. A long chain of them, moving rhythmically, carried away the excavated soil from new foundations, bearing it in baskets on their heads. More than half of them were women. They were the poorest of the poor, but after this hard training in deportment they walked like queens. Their children, in one tattered garment apiece, or none, haunted the open ground and begged vehemently and maliciously from every passer-by.

Two of them converged purposefully upon Dominic, Tossa and Anjli as soon as they stepped out of the taxi. Here were foreigners, their proper prey. A second look at Anjli, as she turned to face them, brought them up standing in considerable doubt; and that was as illuminating for Anjli as for them. And while they were hesitating, a plump lady in a sari came out of the next gate and shooed them indignantly away.

'They are those labourers' children,' she said defensively, in slightly grating English, as though the language had not enough abrasive consonants for her, 'from Orissa. No Punjabi would beg, you please believe me.'

She marched away across the open ground, and the children drew back from her path by a few yards and studied the sky as she went by, to close in again the moment her back was turned, and be shooed away again, good-humouredly enough, by the taxi driver. Dominic paid, and let the car go. He had noticed another taxi stand only a couple of hundred yards away at the corner of the main road.

42

'N 305' said the tablet on the gatepost simply, and there was a small, beautifully-made wooden mail-box attached beneath the number. The wall of the front garden was white, shoulder-high to a man, and the house lay only a few yards back, also white-painted, two storeys high and flat-roofed, with a perforated balustrade, and in the centre of the roof a sort of light pavilion, glazed in from winds and dust-storms, an ideal summer-house for a sociable man who yet had need of a working solitude at times. The ground in front of the house was paved with squares of a grey stone, with narrow flower-beds and a few shrubs along the walls, and a small, decorative tree in a tub by the door. But the enclosure ran round the detached end of the building, and there degenerated into a utilitarian courtyard of beaten earth, with a line for drying washing, and a low wooden shed built into the corner. Beside the shed, under a bracket roof of sacking stretched on a wooden frame, a small brazier burned with a steady glow, and the faint smell of sandalwood and incense was wafted to them in the thin blue smoke. All the fires of Delhi, sacred and profane, seem to contain the evocative scents of worship. Behind the brazier, cross-legged and motionless, sat a lean, shrunken old man, a loose cotton turban on his head, grey hair and tangled beard obscuring most of his face, a brown blanket hugged round his shoulders. When the three strangers came in through the open gate he raised his head, but did not turn in their direction.

At the last moment, with the door before them and the bell-push within reach of a hand, they all hesitated. Felder had talked with blessed bluntness about the moment of truth, about having a roof over Anjli's head that she didn't owe to her father, so that she could meet him on equal terms, and face his acceptance or rejection with unshaken dignity and independence. But when it came to the point, whether she wanted him or not, it was important that he should want her. And there was only one way to find out.

'I'll do it,' said Anjli quickly, and prodded the bell-push with a rose-tipped finger, hard and accurately.

A moment of silence, and then they heard light feet trotting briskly towards the door. Very light feet, naked feet; that characteristic soft slapping of the soles on a stone-paved floor. The door opened, wide to the wall; a revealing gesture, which belongs only to the innocent, open-hearted and generous. A boy of about nineteen, square and sturdy, stood smiling brightly at them across the threshold. He was clean and wide-featured, with close-cropped hair, and wore khaki drill shirt and shorts a size too long for him; handsome muscles bulged the brown arm that held the door open. He bobbed his head repeatedly, and smiled, and said nothing, waiting for them to speak.

'Good morning!' said Dominic, aware of possible non-understanding, but not knowing in the least what to do about it. Names, at any rate, are international currency. 'We are looking for the house of Shri Satyavan Kumar.'

The smile narrowed and wavered. At least he understood English. 'Yes, this is house of Mr Kumar.' His slight frown, his lost look, everything about him but his tongue added: 'But . . . !'

'May we speak with Mr Kumar? He will be expecting us. He has received a letter to tell him that we are coming.'

Nevertheless, Dominic had heard the unspoken 'but', even if he chose to ignore it. It might mean no more than 'but he isn't in at the moment', which would hardly be a catastrophe, even if they were keyed up to meet him immediately, and liable to deflation if kept waiting. Tossa had heard it, too, she was looking more than naturally wise, patient and calm. So had Anjli; her face was a demure mask, no one could tell what went on behind it.

'There is a letter, yes . . .' said the boy slowly. 'But my master not read letter.' His brown eyes wandered from face to face apologetically, as if he might be blamed for this failure of communication. 'The letter is here, I bring it . . .'

'But if we could speak to Mr Kumar,' said Dominic doggedly, 'we can explain everything ourselves.'

'I am sorry. Mr Kumar not here. No one can take letter to him, no one know where can find him. More than one

44

year ago, in the night, Mr Kumar he go away. Never say one word. Never come back.'

After the moment of blank silence, in which the Orissan children advanced their toes over the boundary of the gateway, and the old man behind the brazier shrugged the blanket back a few inches from his shoulders, and the world in general incredibly went on about its business as if nothing had changed, Dominic said in reasonable tones: 'May we come in for a few minutes? You may be able to help us.'

'Please! Memsahib ... missee-sahib ... !' The boy bowed them in gladly, waved them into a small front room, sparsely furnished by western standards, but elegant in tapestries, silks and cushions, and a screen of carved, aromatic wood. The bare feet turned and pattered to the table, where on a silver dish lay an air mail letter. Dorette had wasted her pains.

'Please, here is letter. You take it?'

'No, keep it here,' said Dominic, 'in case Mr Kumar comes home.' But after more than a year without a word, why should he reappear now? And yet this was India, and who knows India's motives and reasons? 'You mean that Mr Kumar simply went away without telling anyone where he was going, or when to expect him back? Not even his mother? His family?' Idiot, there was no other family, of course, he was the only child.

'*Acha*, Sahib. In the night. He did not sleep in his bed, he did not take any luggage, everything left in place. He go. That is all.'

'Like the Lord Buddha,' said Anjli unexpectedly, 'when it was time to depart.' She had a big white canvas handbag on her arm, and Ashok's book inside it; she had been sneaking peeps into the pages even on the taxi ride out here.

'Your father,' Dominic pointed out unwisely, 'was a devout Hindu, by all reports.'

'So was the Lord Buddha,' said Anjli devastatingly. She hadn't been reading to no purpose.

45

'*Father?*' said Satyavan's house-boy, half-dumb with wonder.

'This is Miss Anjli Kumar, Mr Kumar's daughter.'

He joined his hands respectfully under his chin, his brown head bobbing deeply; he did not question her identity, he believed that people told him the truth, as he told them the truth.

'Missee-sahib, I not know anything, I not here when Shri Satyavan go away. When his servants send word to the big house that he gone, my mistress she send them all away, tell me go keep this place until Shri Satyavan return. Nobody see him go, nobody hear. More than one year now, and he send no word.'

'Your mistress?' said Dominic.

'*Acha*, sahib, Shrimati Purnima Kumar. I her house-boy.'

'And there's nobody here now who was here on that night? When Mr Kumar went away?'

'Sahib, no one. Only Arjun Baba.' He said it with the mixture of reverence and indifference that touches, perhaps, only the dead and the mad, both of them out of reach.

'Who is Arjun Baba?'

'The old man. The beggar. Shri Satyavan took him in, and let him live ni the compound. He comes and goes as he will. He eats from our table. Now Shri Satyavan is gone, Shrimati Purnima feeds him. It is all he want. This is his home until he die. Arjun Baba very, very old.'

'But he was here then! He may have heard or seen something ...'

The boy was bowing his head sadly, and sadly smiling. 'Sahib, always he has said he hear nothing, he know nothing. Always, he say this. And, sahib, Arjun Baba is blind.'

It made perfect sense. The old ears pricking, the ancient head turning. But not turning to view. The ear was tuned to them, not the eye. And so old, so very old. And so indebted, in a mutual indebtedness, such as charity hardly knows in the less sophisticated lands of the west. His allegiance belonged only to Satyavan, who if he willed to go

46

must be made free to go. Not all needs are of the flesh.

'Sahib, if you are willing, I think it good you should go to my mistress's house.' He did not say 'to my mistress'; and in a moment it was clear why. 'She very ill, ever since Shri Satyavan go from here she fall sick for him . . .'

'But didn't she try . . .? To get in touch, to find him . . .?'

The young shoulders lifted, acknowledging the sovereignty of individual choice. 'If he must go, he must go. My mistress wait. Only now it is bad with her. But there is Shri Vasudev, Shri Satyavan's cousin. He is manager for family business now. Please, you speak with him.'

'Yes,' said Dominic, 'yes, we will. We have Mrs Kumar's address, we'll go there.'

The boy bowed them anxiously towards the door, and out into the warming sunshine, hovering as though uncertain whether to wish them to stay or go, as though it might rest with him to hold fast Satyavan's daughter, and he might be held answerable if she turned and went away as mysteriously as her father. Anjli halted in the doorway and looked at him thoughtfully.

'You are not from Delhi?'

'No, missee-sahib, I come from a village near Kangra. Shrimati Purnima came from there, and has a house there. My father is her gardener.'

'What is your name?'

'Kishan Singh.' And he pressed his hands together in salute and smiled at her hopefully.

'We shall meet again, Kishan Singh. I am glad you are here to keep my father's house so faithfully and look after Arjun Baba. If you hear any news of him, send it to me at Keen's Hotel. Now we must go to my grandmother.'

Kishan Singh stood at the top of the steps and bowed and smiled her away across the paved garden, in some way reassured; but at the gate she looked back again, and caught Dominic by the arm.

'Wait for me a moment. I want to speak to him . . . the old man. There was nothing wrong with his hearing, I saw that he heard us come.'

47

'We can try,' Dominic agreed doubtfully. 'But it's long odds he doesn't speak English.'

'Kishan Singh did. But let me try, alone...'

Something was changing in Anjli, or perhaps some part of everything in her was changing, her voice, her manner, even her walk. They watched her cross the beaten earth of the yard, and it might almost have been the gliding gait of a woman in a sari, though quite certainly Anjli had never draped a sari round her in her life, and wouldn't know how to set about it even if she had possessed one. She halted before the motionless old man, and though he could not see her, she pressed her hands together in reverence to him, and inclined her head as the boy had done to her.

'Namaste!'

She had no idea how she had known what to say, but when she had said it she knew that it was right. The old head came up, and the sun shone on the sightless face that seemed to gaze at her. A tangle of grey, long hair, beard and brows, out of which jutted a hooked and sinewy nose and two sharp protuberant cheekbones, and a great ridge of forehead. All of his flesh that was visible was the same brown as the brown, dry earth under him. A tremendous remote indifference held him apart from her. The sun gleamed on eyes white and opaque with cataract.

Anjli sat down on her heels, facing him across the little brazier, so that her face was on a level with his. Even before she spoke again, the tilt of his head followed her movement. What his eyes owed him, his ears paid.

'Uncle, I am Satyavan's daughter. I am Anjli Kumar. I have come to find my father. Help me!'

Faintly and distantly a convulsion passed through the fixed, unchanging face, like the passing of a breeze over standing water, and again left it motionless.

'Uncle, you were here, no one but you, when my father went away in the night. If there was a secret he wanted kept from all the world, still he would not have kept it from me.' Did she believe that? She had no time to wonder, she was so sure that the old man heard, considered, understood. He

48

was not deaf and he was not mad, and when she mentioned Satyavan's name the stillness of his face became distant and intense, like a listening stone. He believed her, but he did not know her, and he did not take her word against his own experience for what Satyavan would or would not have done. 'Uncle, now I am going to my grandmother, who also wishes to find my father. If you know anything, where he is, how we can find him, I beg you to tell me.'

He had withdrawn a little into his blanket, his head recoiling into cover from the sun. He said nothing at all; she had the impression that he had turned inwards to converse with himself.

'Come away,' said Dominic gently, his hand on her shoulder. 'You won't get anything out of him.'

She started at the touch, and obediently began to rise, but she did not look up. He *had* understood, and there was something he knew, if his slow and profound communion with himself would allow him to confide it; but not yet, she could see that. Impulsively she rummaged in her bag for something, anything, she could leave with him as a token and a gift in one.

'Uncle, think of me. I am Anjli, his daughter. If you have anything to tell me, send someone – send Kishan Singh – to Keen's Hotel to ask for me. You do understand? You will find me at Keen's Hotel. Kishan Singh will know.' She leaned across the brazier, the faint aromatic smoke tingling in her nostrils, and took the old man's hand in hers, and closed the dry, skinny fingers over her good-luck piece, the mounted gold dollar she sometimes wore as a pendant. 'It is for you. Think of me, and send me word! Namaste!'

She drew back from him resolutely, because she knew she was going to get nothing out of him as yet. But before she turned and walked away through the gate she saw the two ancient hands rise, as though quite independently of whatever mind moved – or immobilised – the worn, inscrutable face, and press themselves together momentarily over her token, in acknowledgement and farewell.

49

'Yes, I've been here,' said Anjli with certainty, as soon as she saw the broad white carriage gates, and the beautifully raked drive curving away between the trees to the distant house that was visible only as a whiteness between the leaves. 'I thought I didn't remember, but now that I see it, I know it's the same. This is where he brought me when I was a little girl.'

'Of course,' said Tossa, 'he wouldn't have the other house then, he was still expecting to stay in America for some years, perhaps even for good. In India this would be his home.'

Anjli passed through the smaller wicket gate with her eyes shut, and walked forward a few steps on the smooth rose-coloured gravel. 'There's a lawn all across the front of the house, and a sort of loggia, with a marble floor. And in the middle of the lawn there's a big fountain.'

There were all these things. There was also a gardener in shorts and drill shirt, dipping water from the fountain basin and watering the flowering shrubs in the scattered round beds, sleeping shrubs only just hinting at budding. Isolated in the emerald green turf, tethered to long, thin snakes of hosing, two sprinklers tirelessly squandered Delhi's precious water supply on preserving the texture and colour and freshness of the Kumar grass.

In a thirsty land privilege can be reckoned in water. Plantation economy, Dominic thought, chilled and daunted, and wondered into what arid byways they had found themselves drawn, aside from the actual life of this painfully real and actual country. It didn't begin with us, he thought, and it hasn't ended with us. We were only an aberration, a contortion of history, suffered almost in its sleep. India twitched a little, and scratched a momentary itch, and that was the coming and the going of the British. But they still have this to reckon with.

'It must be terrible,' said Anjli, suddenly, her fine brows knit in consternation, 'to be so rich!'

As far as they could see, beyond the long, low, pale facade of the house, just coming into view, the artfully

50

spaced trees deployed their varying shapes as decoration, flowers used their colours to punctuate the restful green ground, creamy-white creepers draped the columns of the loggia. Before they reached the curving sweep of the steps that led up to the colonnade and the open double doors within, they had counted five garden boys, watering and tidying and clipping back too assertive leaves, taming and shaping and reducing all things to order. Under the awning of the loggia roof stone urns of flowers were spaced, and out of the open doors a scented smoke filtered. The bell was a looped rope of plaited red silk, but at least there was a bell; they had a means of informing this palace that strangers were on the doorstep, that the outer world did exist.

'I don't want to live here,' Anjli burst out in ill-timed rebellion. In Rabindar Nagar she had looked upon everything, and made no protest, rather advanced a step to look more closely.

'You needn't stay, if you don't want to,' said Dominic, listening to the receding peal of the bell, eddying back and back into the apparently unpeopled recesses of the house. 'We can always take you back with us. Don't worry about anything. But if your grandmother's ill, at least we must enquire about her. And find out if they do know anything here.'

'Yes,' agreed Anjli, strongly recovering, and dug her heels in faithfully at his side.

Someone was coming, hurried, quiet, obsequious feet sliding over polished floors. A turbaned house-man in white cotton, austere but imposing.

'Shri Vasudev Kumar?' said Dominic, evading lingual difficulties.

The man stepped back, and wordlessly waved them inside, into a large hall half-darkened by curtains and palms, and panelled in aromatic dark wood. Far to the rear a staircase spiralled upwards, intricately carved and fretted. The servant bowed himself backwards out of sight through a door to their right, and left them there among the exotics and the impersonal evidences of money and loneliness. Be-

51

yond the staircase the room receded to a large window, and beyond that again they caught a glimpse of a half-circle of paved courtyard, and two large cars standing, and occasionally the passage of scurrying figures. Beneath the civilised quietness there was a deep tremor of agitation.

They waited for some minutes, and then a door opened, somewhere out of sight, and let through the murmur of subdued but troubled voices. Then a man came hurrying in by the door through which the servant had disappeared, and confronted the three visitors with patent astonishment. He was not above medium height, but his hard, stringy Punjabi build made him look taller, and his immaculate western suit of dark grey worsted, and the springy black hair crowning his narrow head, accentuated the impression of length. His complexion was smoothly bronze, his features aquiline, and his age somewhere in the middle thirties. He looked every inch the city magnate, director of companies and arbiter of destinies, but with all his machinery temporarily thrown out of gear. His hands were wiping themselves agitatedly on a silk handkerchief, his thin features jerked with tension, and his eyes, confronted by three such unexpected and unaccountable people, looked dazed and a little demented.

'You wished to see me? I am Vasudev Kumar. But this is a very inconvenient time...' His voice was rather high-pitched, and would have been shrill if he had not been so intent on keeping it almost to an undertone.

'Yes, I see it is, and I'm sorry, Mr Kumar.' Dominic went straight ahead because withdrawal without explanations was now, in any case, out of the question. 'I'll try to be brief, and perhaps we can talk at more leisure another day. We have just come from your cousin's house in Rabindar Nagar, Kishan Singh thought it advisable for us to come straight to you. We realise Mrs Kumar is ill, and certainly don't want to increase your anxieties. My name is Felse, and this is Miss Barber. At her mother's request we've brought your cousin's daughter over to India to join her father, but now we find that he is not in Delhi, and has

52

not received the letter which was sent to him. This is Anjli Kumar.'

That was quite a bombshell, he realised, to drop on anyone, especially at a time when he was already beset by family troubles of another kind; but on the whole Vasudev, by the time he had heard this out to the end, looked considerably less distracted, as though one more shock had served only to concentrate his faculties. He did not, however, look any more friendly. His black, feverish gaze flickered from face to face, and lingered longest on Anjli. He bowed perfunctorily, with no implication of acceptance.

'My cousin's daughter? But we have received no communication about her, we did not expect...'

'No, I realise that. Her mother's letter to Mr Satyavan Kumar is still at his own house, you will find it unopened. I think that will make a better explanation than I can give you. We were expecting simply to bring Anjli over to join her father ... permanently,' he added, seeing no sense in softening anything. 'Naturally none of us had any idea at all that your cousin had vanished a year or more ago. We heard that only this morning, from Kishan Singh. You'll appreciate that in the circumstances the obvious thing to do was to bring Anjli to her grandmother, as her nearest relative here. In any case, Miss Lester had asked us to do that in case of any difficulty arising. But I'm very sorry that we should happen to turn up at such a distressing time for you.'

Anjli, who had stood woodenly to be inspected, not much resenting the suspicion and hostility of a man she didn't know and had no desire to know, asked now in a wary but determined voice: 'Is my grandmother very ill?'

'She has had two strokes since my cousin went away without a word.' Vasudev's high voice clipped the sentence off resentfully; and indeed he had a grievance, having been forced to step in and shoulder the whole abandoned burden of the family businesses, while never quite acquiring the status of managing director in the eyes of any of the Kumar employees and hangers-on. And then, into the bargain, the old lady's illness, with its endless demands upon his patience and his nervous resources. 'Yesterday, I am sorry to say, she had a third one. It is very bad. The doctors have been with her all morning. I do not know what I can do for you ... it is very unfortunate...' A momentary gleam of active suspicion flared in his eyes. 'You can give me proof of the young lady's identity, of course?'

'Of course! She has her own passport, and you can check with the American authorities. There is also her mother's letter waiting to be read.'

'Yes ... yes ... naturally! Please excuse me, but this is so sudden, I can hardly grasp it. And in the circumstances...'

'In the circumstances,' said Dominic, 'having told you the facts, I think we had better leave, and get in touch with you later, when I hope Mrs Kumar will be better. If you have the doctors in the house with her now, we mustn't add to your worries. We are at Keen's Hotel, if you should want to reach us. Otherwise, we'll call you later to enquire about Mrs Kumar.'

Vasudev wrung his hands and twisted the silk handkerchief in a despairing gesture. He did not want them, Dominic thought, upon any terms, but neither was it politic to let them go away like this. There was something more that had to be said, in his own defence, and out it came in a thin, irritated cry: 'It is useless! You have not understood. Mrs Kumar is barely conscious ... paralysed ... she cannot speak... The doctors say that she is dying!'

There was an instant of silence and shock. Then Anjli said, firmly and finally: 'Then I must see her. Whether I stay here or go back to America, I must see her. While there's time. Surely you can see that. I am her granddaughter, and I have a right to see her, and she has a right to see me.'

There was no doubt that Vasudev was distinctly reluctant to allow any such thing, and they were always in some wonder as to why he gave way. For one thing, he had to cover himself. It would have looked bad if he had let an

54

accredited relative go away without knowing that this might be the last chance of seeing Purnima alive, and it would look equally bad if he denied access to the dying woman now that it was requested. But he could have tried persuasion, and in the event he did no such thing. Perhaps there had been something in Anjli's tone that he recognised and respected, an echo of Purnima, the uncompromising firmness of an Indian matriarch laying down the law, very well aware not only of the limitations of her rights (which are obvious) but also of their full scope (which is not, by any means). At any rate, he gave her a narrow, considering look, and then bowed slightly, and turned towards the inner door.

'Very well! Come this way!'

Tossa, following anxiously, murmured: 'Anjli, do you really think ...' But Dominic put his hand on her arm, and whispered: 'Leave her alone.'

Anjli walked rapidly after Vasudev, along a panelled corridor hung with brocades the beauty of which would have stopped her in her tracks at any other time. No wonder they needed legions of servants to run about these endless halls. Door after door, glimpse after glimpse, where the doors were open, of silken luxury; and at the end, a final door, that opened on a dimmed room with a small lamp burning in a corner, and a little garish altar on a shelf behind it, an almanack Krishna, blue and sweetly-smiling, a dressing-table covered not with the brocades of Benares but the tinsel embroidery of the bazaars, a picture of Ramakrishna and another of Vivekananda on the walls, the gentle saintly seed and the hurricane wind that scattered it across the world. And in the middle of the room two white-clad servants standing on one side of a low bed, and on the other side an elderly gentleman of almost completely European appearance, sitting with his fingertips on the patient's pulse.

The bed was just a low wooden frame, without headboard or footboard, with laced springs supporting a thin mattress. A dark blue cloth covered with crude, lovely Naga embroideries of butterflies, elephants, cows and chic-

55

kens, scarcely swelled over the shrunken body beneath it. On the pillow lay a grey head, the still luxuriant hair gathered into a white ribbon; the up-turned face was grey as the hair, one side of the mouth a little twisted, the eyes half-open and fixed. Her hands lay out on the blue coverlet, motionless.

It could have been any Indian woman's room, any but the poorest of the poor. All that wealth and luxury and grace came down at the end into this small, aged figure stretched on a common truckle bed.

Only the eyes were alive. They moved as the strangers came in, the gleam beneath the lids was not quite quenched. They settled upon Anjli.

Anjli went forward slowly, past Vasudev, past the two women, and stood beside the bed. She joined her hands reverently, and bowed her head over them as she had to Arjun Baba; and this time there was a curious suppleness and rhythm about the movement of head and hands which had not been present before.

'Namaste, Grandmother Purnima!'

The fading brightness watched her; there was no other part of Purnima that could express anything now. Anjli slid to her knees beside the bed, to be nearer, and that movement, too, had a fluid certainty about it.

'Grandmother, I am Anjli, your son's daughter. I have come home.'

For one instant it seemed to Dominic and Tossa, watching, that the ancient, burned-out eyes flared feebly, that they acknowledged the stooping girl and approved her. Anjli pressed her joined hands into the Naga coverlet, and laid her face upon them. A tiny, brief convulsion, so infinitesimal that it might almost have been an illusion, heaved at the powerless fingers of Purnima's right hand, moved them a fraction of an inch towards the glossy black head, then let them fall limp. The blue coverlet hung unmoving, subsided, lay still again, and this time finally. The doctor leaned to touch the old woman's eyelid, to reach for her pulse again. One of the women in white began to wail

56

softly and rock herself. Tossa pushed past Dominic, and took Anjli gently by the arm, raising her and drawing her back from the bed.

'Come away now, leave her to them! Come! We'd better go.'

There was no need to tell her that Purnima was dead. Of all the people in the room, Anjli had been the first to know it.

IV

Vasudev overtook them in the loggia, almost running after them with fluttering hands and a dew of sweat on his forehead. The thin line of his black moustache was quivering with agitation.

'Please, one moment! This is terrible ... I do not know how ... I am so sorry ... such a distressing home-coming for my cousin. Let me at least fulfil my responsibilities thus belatedly. You understand, I could hardly believe, so suddenly, with no warning ... Of course Anjli must come to us, this is her home. Allow me, Anjli, to offer you the freedom of this house, until my aunt's estate is settled and proper provision made for you. My aunt's women will take good care of her, Mr Felse, I do assure you. We have an adequate domestic staff. Really, I insist!'

'I couldn't think,' said Dominic very rapidly and very firmly, 'of intruding on the household at this moment, you must allow us to keep Anjli with us at the hotel for a few days. Until after the funeral. You will have your hands quite full until then, and I think it is better that she should not be involved.'

'I am so upset ... so inhospitable and unwelcoming, you must forgive me. Perhaps, however, if you really prefer ...'

'For a few days, until after the funeral, I'm sure it would be better ...'

He was not really sorry to let them go, though insistent on making the offer with all punctilio. Perhaps he was at as great a loss as they were about what to do next. As for Anjli, she walked down the long drive between her temporary guardians, silent and thoughtful, but completely composed. What she had done had been done naturally and candidly, and now there was no more she could do for her grandmother, unless ...

'I suppose funerals happen pretty quickly here, don't they?' she asked practically.

'Not necessarily at this time of year,' Dominic said, accepting this down-to-earth vein as the best bet in the circumstances. 'Maybe I ought to have asked him. I expect there'll be a notice in the papers by this evening, at least about her death.'

'Do you think we should go to the funeral? I know I didn't know her at all, but still she was my grandmother. And she understood what I said to her, I'm sure she did. What do you think, ought we to go?'

'I don't know. I don't know exactly what happens. We might only be in the way, not knowing the drill.'

'I guess we might,' she agreed after due consideration, and sensibly refrained from insisting. And the more he thought about her general behaviour, the more he realised that for years she had been standing squarely on her own feet, for want of mother and father as well as grandmother, and for all her compensatory posturing she had never lost her balance yet.

They walked back to the hotel, for Purnima's house was down in the rich and shady residential roads in the south of town, not far from the golf links, no more than ten minutes' pleasant walking from Keen's. Not one of them said: 'What are we going to do now?' though they were all thinking it.

They waited for the evening papers to arrive, and there it was, the announcement of the death of Shrimati Purnima Kumar, the arrangements for her funeral; imposingly large in the type, as was fitting for so prominent a citizen, and such a rich one. And in every paper alike, at least the English-language ones.

So now they had all the facts flat before them; and while Anjli was taking her bath they could look each other squarely in the face and consider what was to be done.

'We can't possibly leave her here with Cousin Vasudev,' Tossa said.

59

'No, we can't. Of course he may be all right, a thousand to one he is, but with no father here, and no grandmother, and seemingly no wife for Vasudev – I could be wrong, of course, did you get that impression, too?'

'What difference would it make?' said Tossa simply. 'Wife or no wife, we couldn't possibly hand her over to somebody who seems to be next in the running for the family fortune, somebody whose interests, if you look at the thing that way, she definitely threatens. I mean, if Satyavan inherits everything, then even supposing he never turns up, some day they'll have to presume his death, or whatever they do here, and Anjli is next in line. But if there's no Anjli...' She let that trail away doubtfully, and kept her voice low. 'But that's being pretty melodramatic about it, wouldn't you say? He doesn't *look* the wicked-uncle type.'

'No, he doesn't. And I don't suppose they're any more common here than in England, anyhow. And yet, with all these millions of people around, it would be awfully easy for one little one, a stranger, to get sunk without trace. The thing is, unless we find her father, then the next move is Dorette's responsibility, not ours, and we've no right to appropriate it to ourselves.'

'Dorette,' said Tossa with awful certainty, 'would dump her on Vasudev and never think twice.'

'Maybe she would, but she isn't going to do it by proxy. Not these proxies, anyhow.'

'Hear, hear! So what *do* we do?'

'I tell you what, I think we'd better ring up Felder and ask his advice. After all, he did offer to help.'

When he got through to the villa near Hauz Khas, it was Ashok Kabir who answered the telephone.

'They're not in yet, they'll probably be late. And they're off to Benares early in the morning. Is it urgent? Why not tell me, and I'll pass the problem on to him and ask him to call you back when he does get in?'

Dominic told him the whole story of Satyavan's defection and Purnima's death, down to the last detail that seemed relevant, and then sat down, a little cheered by

60

Ashtok's evident concern and sympathy, to wait for Felder to call him back. Presently Anjli sauntered in from the bathroom of the suite she shared with Tossa. In a flowing cotton dressing-gown, and with her black hair swirling softly round her shoulders, for the first time she looked Indian.

'Watch your step when you go for your bath, Tossa, we've been invaded. Two huge cockroaches – I suppose they come up the plumbing. Put the light on five minutes before you go to run your bath, and I bet they'll take the hint and run for the exit.' She was being, perhaps, deliberately cooler than she felt about these hazards, just as she probably was about her experiences of the morning; but the slight over-statement was merely that, not a falsification. Presented with a burden, she practised the best way of carrying it. Confronted by a problem, she would walk all round it and consider how best to grapple with it. They were beginning to understand their Anjli.

'That's nothing,' said Tossa, 'a gecko fell on me this morning in bed.'

'I know, I heard you squeal. There's another one going to fall on you any minute now.' He was clinging with his tiny, splayed feet to the high ceiling just above Tossa's head, close to the light fixture, lying in wait for flies, a whitish green lizard no more than four inches long, of which more than half was tail. He was so young and small that he was still almost translucent, and only the faint, rapid palpitation of his throat indicated that he was alive, and not a worked fragment of alabaster. 'I'd rather have geckos than cockroaches, any day. Anything with up to four legs,' said Anjli, quite seriously, 'is my brother. Over four, and they're out.'

'What about snakes?'

'Things with no legs are out, too. But not as way out as things with eight. Who was it on the phone? Cousin Vasudev?'

'I called Mr Felder,' said Dominic, 'but he wasn't back from shooting yet. They're going to ask him to call back.' No need to tell her the voice on the phone had belonged to

Ashok Kabir; she would have resented being left in ignorance, even in the bath.

It was another hour before Felder's call came through. Anjli was in bed by then, but with her nose buried in *The Life of the Budda*, and at the first ring she was out and streaking for Dominic's sitting-room door. The conversation was brief, and apparently satisfactory.

'Of course!' said Dominic, heaving a vast breath of relief. 'How very simple you make it sound! Thanks a-lot, that's what we'll do.'

'And let me know what happens, will you do that? I shall be worrying about that kid from now on until I know, but I'm betting you it will bring results, all right. For the next few days you can get me at Clark's Hotel, Benares – OK?'

'OK, and thanks again. Hope everything will go right with the shooting.'

'Now you're believing in miracles! Never mind, it's gone well today. And you take those girls and have a look at Delhi, don't waste a minute. So long, then, I'll be hearing from you!'

He was gone, energetic and bracing as ever, leaving his effect behind like a potent wine. Dominic hung up, relaxed and grateful.

'What did he say?' They were both at him in a moment, one on either side. '*What's* so simple?'

'He says, with Mrs Kumar's death notice plastered all over the evening press – and you can bet it will be in the dailies tomorrow, too, – Satyavan will be absolutely certain to see it, wherever he is, and he'll come running to pick up his responsibilities. No son will let anyone else run his mother's funeral. All we've got to do is sit back and wait, to see if your father turns up for the ceremony. And the odds are strongly that he will.'

Nobody said – nobody even thought, in the exhilaration of the moment – '*if he can!*'

For two days they were on equal terms with all the other carefree European tourists in Delhi. They walked about the

62

busy shopping streets round Connaught Place until their feet ached. They proceeded, half-stunned with grandeur, the full length of the King's Way from India Gate to Rashtrapati Bhavan, once the Viceroy's palace, now the residence of the President of India, with its two great flanking blocks of the government secretariat, vast, glowing pink sandstone, one of the better legacies of the Raj, along with the legal system and the indomitable Indian railways. They risked their lives in the hailstorm of bicycles as the clerks of Delhi streamed to work in the morning rush hour, and baked themselves brown in the midday sun in the silent green park among the Lodi tombs, close to their own hotel. Islam weighted India with vast and splendid elegies to death, India herself withdrew elusively, dissolving into ash and essence, leaving life to speak for itself. And so it did, in the children who mobbed the strangers in Purana Quila, the Old Fort, half glorious ruined monument to the past, half refugee village congealed into permanence for want of other quarters; in the magical glimpses of Old Delhi after dark, blanketed figures squatting by stalls half-lit with tiny smoky lanterns, twilight children cross-legged, suddenly mute and inscrutable as gods, and everywhere smoky scents of cowdung and joss and jasmine and sweat and all-pervading aromatic dust, electric on the darkness.

They took a motor-cycle rickshaw out to the Qutb Minar and the enormous ruined city of Tuqhluquabad, south of Delhi, silent and wonderfully peaceful within its broken, giant wall; and from there, having picnicked at ease in the sun, they crossed the road to the tightly-walled enclosure of the domed tomb of Ghias-ud-Din Tuqhluq, compressed as a blockhouse yet beautifully-proportioned, red walls leaning into themselves as solidly as the Egyptian Pyramids, white dome rearing austerely just high enough to peer over the flat brown plain, sprinkled with meagre trees.

They took a taxi to Humanyun's tomb, the resting-place of the second Mogul emperor, delicately attached to the eastern flank of Delhi in an immaculate formal garden. They had no idea that they were looking at something in its own way fully as beautiful as the Taj, which on this visit they could hardly hope to see; nevertheless, their hearts lifted strangely as they looked at the long, level, red terrace, the jut of mellow stonework above, and the poised and tranquil white dome. No floating off, balloon-wise, here, this was a tethered dream, with feet rooted in the ground. At the gate, as they left, a bearded snake-charmer, grinning ingratiatingly, coaxed out of its basket a dull, swaying brown cobra. Everything about it was pathetic, nothing was sinister, except for the single flick of its forked tongue; almost certainly it had no poison-sacs. They wondered if the music enchanted or hurt; there was no way of knowing. They paid their few new pice, and took their taxi back north to the Red Fort to lose count of time wondering among the white marble palaces and the paradisal gardens that overlook the Yamuna river. The complex waterways in the gardens were still dry at this time of year, and the fountains silent, but with a little imagination they could insert a small, lighted lamp into every niche in the lattices of stone where the water-level dropped, and see the silver curve of falling water lit from within and giving off rainbows like the scintillations from a diamond. The Moguls loved water, played with it, decorated their houses with it, built sumptuous pavilions in which to bathe in it, and took it to bed with them in little marble channels and lotus-flower fountains to sing them to sleep.

From this haunted palace in its dignity and quietness the three tourists plunged straight into the broad, teeming, over-peopled clamour of the Chandni Chowk, Old Delhi's grand market-place, screaming with cinema posters and advertisement hoardings, shrill with gossiping citizens and hurrying shoppers. They peered into the deep, narrow, open shops to see the silks and cottons baled and draped in unimaginable quantity, the Kashmiri shawls fine as cobweb, the gold and silver jewellery and the cheap glass bangles, the nuts and seeds and spices, the unknown vegetables, the fantastic sweetmeats. Horse-drawn tongas, scooter-rickshaws, cars, bicycles, stray dogs, pedestrians, all mingled in the roadway

64

in a complicated and hair-raising dance. The noise was deafening. So next, because according to the map they were less than a mile from it and could easily walk there, they went to Rajghat, the spot close to the river bank where Mahatma Gandhi's body was burned after his assassination, and where now a white balustrade encloses a paved space and a flower-covered dais. And there, though there were plenty of people, there was silence.

At the end of the first day they half expected that Cousin Vasudev would telephone or send them a note, either to follow up his tentative recognition of Anjli's identity and admit his own family responsibility for her, or to effect a careful withdrawal and leave the whole thing in abeyance, pending legal consultations. But there was no message.

'I suppose he has got his hands full,' Tossa said dubiously. 'And after all, he is only a cousin, and you could hardly hold him responsible as long as we've got Dorette to go back to, could you?'

'I expect,' said Anjli cynically, 'he's just holding his breath and keeping his eyes shut in the hope that if he doesn't look at us or speak to us we'll go away.'

On the second evening there was still no message. They had spent the afternoon prowling round all the government and state shops in New Delhi, among the leathers and silks and cottons and silverware and copperware and ivory carvings, well away from the banks of the Yamuna where the rites of death are celebrated. Nobody mentioned funerals. Everybody thought privately of the little, shrunken body that had hardly swelled the bedclothes, swathed now in white cotton for the last bath and the last fire. By the time they came back to Keen's Hotel, after a Chinese meal at Nirula's, Purnima was ash and spirit.

And there was no message for them at the desk, and no one had telephoned.

'Maybe he's got a whole party of funeral guests on his hands still,' said Tossa, 'and hasn't had time to think about us yet. I don't know what happens, there may be family customs ... I know there don't seem to be any more near

65

relatives, but there must be some distant ones around somewhere ... and then all the business connections, with a
family like that ...'

'We've got to find out,' said Dominic. 'I'd better ring
him, if he won't ring us.'

He made the call from their own sitting-room upstairs. A
high, harassed voice answered in Hindi, and after a wait of
some minutes Cousin Vasudev's agitated English flooded
Dominic's ear with salutations, apologies and protestations,
effusive with goodwill but fretful with weariness and hag-
ridden with responsibilities.

'It is unfilial, one cannot understand such behaviour.
Everything I have had to do myself, everything. And into the
bargain, with these newspapermen giving me no peace....
It is a decadent time, Mr Felse, in all countries of the world
duties are shirked, family ties neglected ... The old order
breaks down, and nothing is sacred any longer. What can
we do? It is left for the dutiful to carry other people's
burdens as well as their own ...'

It seemed that Dominic's question had not merely
answered itself, somewhere in the flood of words, but also
been washed clean away on the tide. Nevertheless, when he
could get a word in he asked it.

'Do you mean that Anjli's father has not come home?
Not even for the funeral?'

'He has not. Everything is left to me. One cannot understand how a son could ...'

'And he hasn't written, either? After all, he might be
abroad somewhere ...'

'I assure you, Mr Felse, certain preliminaries are necessary before Indian citizens go abroad. The authorities
would know if that was the case, and of course I did, very
discreetly, you understand ... strictly private enquiries ...
My aunt did not wish it, but I felt it to be my duty ... No,
there has been no word from him at all. The position as far
as that is concerned is quite unchanged ...'

Dominic extricated himself from the current, made the
best farewells he could, and hung up the receiver. They

66

looked at one another, and for some minutes thought and were silent. Not because they had nothing to say, but because what was uppermost in two minds was not to be expressed in front of Anjli. Why, thought Dominic blankly, did it never occur to us until now to wonder whether he really did go of his own will? And whether there might not be a completely final reason why he hasn't come back? And has that really never occurred to Cousin Vasudev, either? In all this time, and with that much money at stake?

'He may not have seen the papers at all,' said Tossa sturdily. 'I know people in England who almost never look at the things.'

'He *can't* have seen them,' amended Anjli with emphasis, 'or he'd be here.'

'But what do we do now? We could hang on for a few days longer, certainly, maybe even a couple of weeks, but if he's as unavailable as all that what difference will two weeks make? And in any case, that would be a gamble, because we can't do that *and* pay for a single ticket back to London for Anjli. So we've got to make up our minds right now.'

Anjli dropped the tiny packet of damp tissue-paper she was just unwrapping, and gaped at him in consternation for a moment; but she was quick to recover her own reticence, which in some unquestioned way had become curiously precious to her here in Delhi.

'You mean you want me to go back to England with you?' she said with composure.

'What else can we possibly do?' said Dominic reasonably. 'We can't deliver you to your father, which was the object of the exercise, or to your grandmother, which would have done as a substitute. The only legal guardian you have is your mother – for the time being, at any rate. I don't see any alternative but to take you back with us ... do you?'

'We could go and stay at Grandmother Purnima's house for a while, at any rate. He did ask us. That way, we needn't pay hotel bills, and we'd still have enough for my ticket back if it came to that in the end.'

'*We* couldn't. He didn't ask us, he asked *you*. And you said you didn't want to live there. And in any case,' said Dominic, smiling at her ruefully, 'you don't suppose we'd really hand you over to a man we don't know at all, and just fly off and leave you, do you?'

She owned, after a moment's thought, that that was too much to expect of them. 'Well, all right, then, what's the answer?' But she knew, and she knew he was right, by his standards and by hers. Somehow standards seemed irrelevant to this new world; what governed action was something just as valid and moral, but more inward, and not to be discussed or questioned. She picked up the little moist packet, and carefully unwrapped the exquisite bracelet of white jasmine buds Dominic had bought her in Chandni Chowk, strung neatly on green silk cord the colour of the stems. 'Tie it on, would you, please?'

Three days ago Dominic would have suspected that confiding gesture of her wrist towards him, and the way she inclined her head over the dewy trifle as he tied the green cord. Now she seemed three years older than her age, and every touch and sound and look of hers he accepted as genuine. She turned her wrist, leaning back to admire. 'They wear them in their hair, don't they? I could do that, too, if I put mine up, there's plenty of it. A big knot on the back of my neck, like this, and the bracelet tied round the knot ... Imagine all those gorgeous flowers, in winter! Did you ever see such gardens?'

'The answer,' Tossa said, watching the two of them with a faintly ironic smile, 'is that we all go back to London. There's nothing else we can do. We'll have to see about your ticket and the flight in the morning.'

'You're the boss,' said Anjli. 'All right, if you say so, that's what we do. Now, if you folks don't mind, I'm going to put our bathroom light on and alert the enemy to get right out of there, and in about five minutes I'm going to have my bath.'

She had to go out into the corridor to go to the suite she

shared with Tossa, next door; and in the corridor she met
her least favourite room-boy, bearing on a pretentious in-
laid tray a very grubby folded scrap of paper. His grin – it
was a curious side-long grin, the antithesis of Kishan
Singh's radiant beam, and his eyes never met hers for more
than a fraction of a second, but slid away like quicksilver –
convulsed his thin dark face at sight of her, and he bowed
himself the remaining four yards towards her, and proffered
the tray.

'Missee-sahib, messenger he bring this for you. Say,
please, give privately. Your room dark, I think perhaps
better wait ...'

He had a confiding, you-and-I-understand-each-other
voice and manner. She hadn't been a film star's daughter all
her life without meeting his like in many different places.
She dropped a quarter-rupee on the tray and picked up the
dirty little note with more curiosity than she showed.

'Thank you! That's all!'

He withdrew backwards, not out of extreme humility,
but to watch her face and bearing as she opened and read
the note; which got him nothing, for she didn't open and
read it until she had stared him into turning and slithering
away towards the stairs. Then she had it open in an instant,
and held under the light in the corridor. She could see there
was no more than one line to read; a glance, and she had it
memorised.

English characters sprawled shapelessly and shakily
across the paper, the pencil now pressing, now feebly touch-
ing, an old man's hand:

'Daughter, come morning before light alone.'

She had unfolded it so hurriedly that something small
had fallen from it at her feet. She picked it up, and her
fingers knew it before ever she got it raised to the light. It
was her gold dollar, the token she had given to Arjun Baba
in the courtyard of her father's house in Rabindar Nagar.

The room-boy was on the stairs when she caught up with
him. There was no time to be diplomatic; instinct told her,
instead, to be autocratic. And, given co-operation, generous.

'Boy!' He turned, responsive to the tone, with more alacrity than usual. 'Who brought this note?'

'A messenger, missee-sahib!' The obsequious shoulders lifted eloquently. 'Perhaps a porter? Or he could be somebody's office peon. In a red head-cloth, like a porter.'

'And he left no other message? Just brought the note? How long ago?'

'Missee-sahib, only this minute. I come upstairs, your room in darkness, when I see you come ... That peon maybe still only in courtyard there ...'

Of course, there was no other way out. To enter Keen's you must thread a narrow archway in from the street, walk round a high hedge and so come into the interior court; and if driving a car, you must drive from a double gate higher up the street, right round one wing to the same paved patio. Anjli dropped half a rupee on to her least favourite room-boy's tray, and turned and ran from him without concealment, straight to the landing window that gave on to the courtyard gallery. Creepers wreathed the outline of the night in feathery leaves. Down below, lights shone upon the white paving and the scattered shrubs in their huge ceramic pots. Away across the expanse of silver-washed whiteness, towards the enclosing dark of the high box hedge, a fore-shortened figure strolled at leisure, but still briskly, for the night air was sharp to the edge of frost. Under the last of the lights she saw the extravagantly-tied, wide-bowed headcloth, faded red. Like an office peon! She did not know the term, but she understood what it meant. The more menial the function, the more compensatory the uniform. On the whole not a bad principle. But Arjun Baba had no office peon to run his errands, and this was not Kishan Singh. Perhaps a kind neighbour with a job in the city. Perhaps a public porter earning a few extra pice and acquiring merit.

The man below her – he was rounding the corner of the box hedge now – was whistling. The notes came up to her clearly in the almost frosty air and the nocturnal stillness. She followed them subconsciously, plaintive notes

70

rising, turning, falling, simple and poignant, like a folk-tune. She caught herself picking up the cadence accurately before she realised what she was hearing.

But it was impossible! No, that was nonsense, she knew what she was hearing, once the memory fell into place. But how was it possible, then? 'Siddhartha' wasn't anything like finished yet, not even the shooting. The music had certainly not yet been recorded. How could a street porter or an office messenger know the entire air of Yashodhara's bereaved lullaby, the simplified theme of the Buddha's morning raga?

Leaning over the rail of his balcony, Dominic pricked up his ears abruptly, listening.

'Hey, did you hear that? Listen!'

'Somebody whistling,' said Tossa, unimpressed, 'that's all. They do it even here. You remember, Ashok said...'

'Hush!'

She hushed obediently; he was very serious about it. She held her breath, following the tiny, silvery trail of notes up and down, a curiously rueful air. It receded, suddenly muted by the high hedge, but still heard, growing clearer again for a while as the angle changed, then cut off finally by the bulk of the wing. Now he must be in the street, lost among the trees. Theirs was a select residential road, silent at night. Indian cities have their preserves of silence, even close to the hub and the heart.

'Did you hear it? Did you get it?'

'I heard him whistling,' she said wonderingly. 'What about it?'

'You didn't get what it was he was whistling?' And Dominic picked up the air himself, and whistled it softly in his turn; he had an ear for a tune even at first hearing. 'You don't recognise it? But was it the same? The same as his?'

'I think so. It sounds the same. Why? How did you know it?'

'I heard it the other day, and so did you. It's the song from Ashok's music to the film, don't you remember? The

71

simple one, the one Kamala sings. He *said* he'd be disappointed if they weren't whistling it in the streets before long. But not before the film's released! What on earth's going on?'

'But are you sure?' she asked doubtfully. 'After all, the ragas are everybody's property, you just take them and improvise on them, don't you? Somebody could accidentally produce a tune that recalled Ashok's, couldn't he? I mean, the unit is in Sarnath – or back in Clark's Hotel at Benares, probably, at this hour. Not in Delhi, anyhow.'

'I know. I must be imagining things,' agreed Dominic, shivering, and turned back from the staring stars into the warmth of the room.

V

Anjli arose in the early hours of the morning, and stood beside her bed for a little while, listening to the silence, which was absolute. Not even a stirring of wind in the trees outside the open window. The air was clear, still and piercing, like dry wine.

She was just getting used to the size of the room, which held two beds, and could have accommodated ten. The distance between her single bed and Tossa's made movement easy and safe. She dressed with care and deliberation, because she had the deep conviction within her that she was not coming back, that she had better get everything right the first time, for there was not going to be any chance of revising measures once taken. Delhi would be as cool as an English spring for some weeks yet, the nights cold, midday perhaps reaching summer warmth in the sun. Better be prepared for all temperatures. She put on the lambswool and angora suit in muted strawberry pink, took a scarf and her light wool coat, and slipped her feet into supple walking shoes. Then she carefully tucked into her large handbag a cotton dress, sandals, toilet necessaries and a towel. That was all. The Lord Buddha, when he passed through the palace gardens among the oblivious sleepers, carried nothing but what he wore, and even that he gave away when he entered the outer world and sent Channa back with the weeping white horse Kantaka.

She had some money of her own, changed into rupees for shopping, and some travellers' cheques. Her passport, her own personal papers – it seemed wrong to possess any of these. But she was living in this present world, and its customs were not those of Kapilavastu, and a certain respect was due to the laws of the land. So she allowed herself the money and the credentials. And at the last moment she turned back to her dressing-table, and painstakingly tied round her left wrist the slightly wilted bracelet of jasmine buds. Dominic was, after all, rather sweet, and it wasn't like allowing oneself real jewels. The Lord Buddha had divested himself of all his jewels before he exchanged his rich silk robes for a huntsman's homespun tunic in the woods. Maybe she could exchange her expensive cardigan suit for shalwar and kameez and a floating, infuriating gauze scarf, such as the schoolgirls wore. She peered into the dark mirror, where a faint cadence of movement indicated the ghost of Anjli peering back at her, and imagined the transformation.

In the other bed Tossa slept peacefully. She never stirred when the door of the room was gently opened. Anjli looked back, and was reassured, and at the same time curiously touched. She hadn't expected much from Tossa, to tell the truth; anyone her mother deputed to do her dirty work for her was automatically suspect. But Tossa had been a surprise; so quiet, and so reasonable, and so aware, as if she knew just what was going on. Which was nonsense, because there couldn't really be two Dorettes, could there? And how else would she know? Not stupid, either, she could put her foot down gently but finally when she liked. Anjli hoped they would not feel too responsible, and that she would soon be able to get in touch with them and put their minds at rest. Also that they would spend the last dollar of Dorette's money on seeing India before they went back to England.

The corridor was lit only by a small lamp at the end. No one was moving. She listened, and the whole house seemed to be one silence. Anjli closed the door of the room softly behind her, and tiptoed along the darker wall towards the landing window that led to the balconies. There was a stairway to the courtyard there; and there were no gates or doors closing the archway that opened into the street. She knew the lie of the land by now; by the carriage gates farther along there were always a few rickshaws and taxis hopefully waiting, even at night.

74

She was not going back to Dorette's synthetic world. Not now, nor ever. There were plenty of things in India that she didn't want, the cockroaches, the flies, the dirt, the lean, mad-looking tonga horses, half-demented with overwork and rough usage, the maimed animals that no one was profane enough to kill but no one was vulnerable enough to pity, the hunger, the disease, the monumental indifference. Nevertheless, India was all she wanted, India and the links that bound her to it, notably her father, the indispensable link.

There was a room-boy curled up asleep in the service box at the end of the corridor. She passed him by silently, and he slept on. Down the stairs into the courtyard she went, and from shadow to shadow of the spaced trees across to the end of the box hedge – perhaps it wasn't box, but it looked like it, and that was how she thought of it – and round it into comparative security. Now there was only the porter's box by the archway. They were asleep there, too. She stole past them like a ghost, and never troubled their dreams. She was in the street, melting into the shelter of the trees, alone in the faintly lambent darkness.

She thought of the receding red turban, and the fine thread of melody whistled across the evening air to her, like an omen; it no longer troubled her, it was inevitably right now, at this hour. The early morning, and the guests – the guest! – departing . . .

At the last moment she thought better of taking a rickshaw from the end of the carriage drive, though there were two standing there. She crossed the road, instead, and circled round them, keeping in the shelter of the trees; for when enquiries began to be made about her departure, these would surely be the first people to be questioned. Close to the southern end of Janpath was Claridge's Hotel, and there would just as surely be a taxi or two waiting there.

There was one car, the Sikh driver asleep behind the wheel, and one cycle-rickshaw, with a lean brown boy curled up in a blanket inside the high, shell-shaped car-

75

riage. Anjli chose the rickshaw. It would take longer to get her out to the edge of town, but it would pass silently everywhere, and not be noticed. It would be cheaper, too, and she might yet need her money. Who knew how far she would have to travel to find her father, even if Arjun Baba could tell her the way?

The boy awoke in a flash, uncurling long, thin limbs like a startled spider, and baring white teeth in a nervous grin.

'Will you take me,' said Anjli, low-voiced, 'to the new school in Rabindar Nagar?' She could have given the number of the house and been dropped at the door, but the hunt for her, if pursued devotedly enough, might even turn up this boy; and besides, if her father's secret was so urgent, she did not want any witnesses.

The boy bowed and nodded her into the carriage, and pushed his cycle off silently into the roadway. It was a long drive, she knew, perhaps a little over two miles, but she was a lightweight, and the bicycle was new and well-kept; it would still be practically dark when they arrived. The shapes of New Delhi flowed past her mutely in the dimness, trees and buildings, occasionally a glimpse of a man stumbling to work, still half-sleeping, sometimes the smoky glimmer of little lanterns attached to the shacks where vegetable-sellers slept beside their stalls, waiting to unload the goods brought in at dawn. The stars were still visible, silver sewn into velvet. Now they were out of the city and cruising along the airy terrace of the Ridge for a while, where the air was sharp and bitterly cold, dry and penetrating as the sands from which it blew. And now the first small white villas, making pale patterns against the smoke-coloured earth that would be tawny by day.

The boy halted obediently at the shiny new gates of the school, and asked no questions. Probably he had no English, for he said not a word throughout the transaction, though he must have understood enough to bring her where she wished to be. When she opened her bag they needed no words. He had already summed up her appearance, her clothing and her innocence, perhaps even over-estimating

76

the innocence. He smiled at her beguilingly, and deprecatingly raised two fingers. He thought she didn't know exactly how many new pice per mile he was supposed to charge; but her mind was on other things, and in any case her mood was that of one turning her back upon the world's goods. She gave him his two rupees, and it was a good investment, for he promptly mounted his cycle and rode away before she could change her mind. So he never saw which way she turned from the school.

Only a hundred yards to go now. It was still almost fully dark, only the faintest of pallors showed along the horizon, transforming the sky into an inverted bowl of black rice-grain porcelain with a thin golden rim. She saw the shape of Satyavan's house rise along the sky-line ahead, the only one with that little princely pavilion on the roof; she wondered for a moment if he had a garden up there, or at least small decorative trees in tubs, like the one beside the front door below. All the whites of the white walls were a shadowy, lambent grey, for as yet there were no colours, only cardboard forms, not solids but merely planes. She came to the gate of filigree iron, and for a moment wondered what she would do if it turned out to be locked or chained; but the latch gave to her hand soundlessly. At the end of the garden wall, drawn aside from the roadway, a small van sat parked in the worn, straw-pale grass. Did that mean that someone had come home? Or was it merely the property of the man next door, the plump lady's husband, who was probably a travelling salesman, or a veterinary surgeon, or something else modestly professional with need of transport?

She let herself into the compound. The house was dark and quiet, and Kishan Singh, with no need to rise early, was surely still fast asleep. But in the distant corner of the earth yard a small gleam of light shone, and the now familiar scent of dust and humanity and incense, funereal, vital and holy, stung her nostrils as she tiptoed across the front garden.

In front of his corner kennel, under his lean-to roof,

Arjun Baba sat just as she had seen him three days ago, huddled in his brown blanket against the night's cold, peering down sightlessly into the minute flame of his brazier. A glossy red reflection picked out the jut of cheek-bones and brow from the tangle of grey hair and beard that hid his face. When he heard her step he raised his head, but did not turn towards her. She had a feeling that three days had been lost, and all that had passed in them was a fantasy, not a reality; or perhaps that those three days had been demanded of her as a probation for what was still to come. Perhaps he had not even expected her. Yet she was here.

She crossed the few yards of bare, beaten earth with the soft, gliding walk of a woman in a sari, and sank to her heels, squatting to face him across the brazier.

'Namaste! Uncle, I am Anjli Kumar. You called me, I have come.'

The old man shifted slowly in his blanket, and linked his hands beneath his chin in greeting. A creaking voice blew through the tangle of grey hair and said hoarsely: 'Namaste!'

'Uncle, you have something to tell me?'

The ancient head wagged in the ambiguous manner she had learned to interpret as: Yes. Slowly he shrugged back the blanket from his shoulders, and lifted his eyes to her face.

It was the gleam of the brazier that warned her. She had braced herself unconsciously to contemplate once again the opaque white membrane of cataract filming over the sightless eyes, and instead there was a bright darkness with a hard golden high-light, the sharp pheasant-stare of eyes that saw her very clearly. For an instant she stared back transfixed and motionless; then without a sound she recoiled from him and sprang to her feet, whirling on one heel to run like a deer.

A hand reached out across the brazier and caught her by the long black braid of hair, dragging her back. She opened her lips to cry out, but the blanket was flung over her head, and hard fingers clamped the dusty folds tightly over her mouth and nostrils, ramming the cloth between her teeth. A long arm gripped her round the waist and swung her off her feet, and in a moment she felt something drawn tightly round her arms above the elbow, pinning them fast. She tried to kick, and the voluminous folds of the blanket were drawn close and tied, muffling every movement. A hand felt for her mouth, thrust the woollen stuff in deep, and twisted a strip of cloth round her head to fasten the gagging folds in place.

The hair-line of gold along the horizon had thickened into a pale-rose-coloured cord. Just before the first back-door tradesman pushed his hand-cart into the alley between the houses, the little van parked on the grass started up, and was driven decorously away towards the main road.

VI

Dominic awakened to an insistent tapping at his door about eight o'clock, to find the room flooded with sunlight. He rolled out of bed and reached for his dressing-gown so abruptly that one gecko, until then apparently petrified in a corner of the ceiling, whisked out of sight under the rickety wiring, and another, prowling within inches of Dominic's heel as he hit the floor, shot away in a fright, leaving behind on the boards a two-and-a-half inch tail that continued to twitch for ten minutes after its owner had departed.

'Dominic, are you awake? It's me, Tossa. Open the door!' She fell into the room in a cloud of nylon ruffles. 'You haven't seen anything of Anjli, have you?' A silly question, she realised, his eyes were barely open yet. 'She's gone! I woke up a little while ago, and she isn't anywhere to be seen, and her bed's cold. I thought at first she was in the bathroom, but she isn't. Her pyjamas are there folded on the pillow. But *she's gone!*'

Her glance fell upon the wriggling tail at that moment, and her eyes opened wide in incredulous horror, for she had read about, but never yet encountered, the more unnerving habits of the smaller lizards. But she was too preoccupied to spare a word for the phenomenon Dominic plainly had not even noticed.

'It's a fine morning,' he said reasonably, 'she'll have gone off for a walk. I don't suppose she's any farther away than the garden.'

Tossa shook her head emphatically. 'She's taken that outsize handbag of hers. I checked as soon as I realised... It's got all her money in it, and her passport. Her coat's gone from the wardrobe, and a cotton dress ... and her washing things have vanished out of the bathroom. No, she's up to something on her own. Whatever it is, she planned it herself. You know what I think? I'd have sworn even at the time she was being too quiet and reasonable. When it came to the point, she simply didn't want to go back home.'

'But she surely wouldn't run off on her own, just to give us the slip? She's got nobody here to turn to, after all, even if she does hate the thought of going back to England.'

'She's got a cousin,' Tossa reminded him dubiously.

'She didn't show much sign of taking to him.'

'I know. But he's the only relative she has got left over here, as far as we know. We'd better try there first, hadn't we?' Her eyes remained fixed on the abandoned tail, now twitching solemnly and regularly as a metronome. Her toes curled with horror. 'Don't step back!' she warned; his bare foot was just an inch from the pale-green tip.

Dominic looked down, uttered a startled yelp, and removed himself several feet from the improbable thing in one leap. 'Good lord, what on earth ... ! *I* haven't done that, surely? I swear I never touched ...

'They say they do it when they're scared,' said Tossa, and wondered if she had not shed an appendage herself this morning, a taken-for-granted tail of European self-confidence and security. 'I think they grow another. She can't really have gone off and left us permanently, can she? Surely she'd be afraid!'

'Go and get dressed, and we'll see if she comes to breakfast. If not, maybe some of the hotel staff will have seen her go out.'

That was good sense, and Tossa seized on it gratefully; Anjli had a healthy appetite, and was always on time for meals. But this time the magic did not work. The two of them met at their table in the ground-floor dining-room, the garden bright and empty outside the long windows; the tea arrived, strong and dark as always, the toast, the eggs; but no Anjli.

They went in search of the room-boy. Last night's attendant was off-duty for the day, and the shy southerner who had just tidied away the gecko's tail, finally limp and still, had seen nothing of Miss Kumar. Nor had the sweeper in the courtyard, nor the porters at the gates. All this time Dominic had had one eye cocked for the truant's return, fully expecting her to saunter in from a walk at any moment; but time ticked by and the possible sources of information dried up one by one, and still no Anjli. By a process of elimination they arrived at the reception clerk, who was hardly a promising prospect, since he had come on duty only at eight o'clock this morning, when Anjli's absence had already been discovered. However, they tried.

'Miss Kumar? No, I have not seen her this morning, I am sorry.' The clerk was a dapper young man, friendly and willing to please. He looked from one anxious face to the other, and grasped that this was serious; and it was in pure kindness of heart that he felt impelled to add something more, even if it was of no practical help. 'I have seen nothing of her since she came in with you yesterday evening. To be sure, I remember there was a note delivered here for her later...'

'Note?' said Dominic, pricking up his ears. He looked at Tossa, and she shook her head; not a word had been said about any note. 'Did she get it?'

'Of course, sir, I sent it up to her as soon as it came, by the room-boy.'

'You don't know who it was from? Who brought it?' Certainly not the postman, at that hour.

'No, sir, I cannot say from whom it came. It was a common peon who brought it, some shop porter, perhaps. Though I do recall that the note was not in an envelope, but just a sheet of paper folded together – a little soiled, even...'

It did not sound at all like the immaculate Vasudev. And who else was there in Delhi to be sending notes to Anjli? The film unit was away in Benares, and no one else knew her.

'About what time was this?'

'I cannot say precisely, sir, but a little after nine, probably.'

Anjli had announced her intention of going for her bath at about that hour. And only a few minutes later, that floating wisp of melody had drifted in at the window that overlooked the courtyard ... No, he was imagining connections where there were none. Tossa was right, the ragas were there for everyone to use and enjoy. It was placing too much reliance on his unpractised ear to insist that what he had heard was not merely Raga Aheer Bhairab, but Ashok's unique folksong variation of it, and no other.

So they were back to the necessity of beginning the hunt for Anjli somewhere; and the obvious place was Purnima's house. Where, of course, they told each other bracingly in the taxi, Anjli would certainly be.

'Note?' Vasudev's thin black moustache quivered with consternation. 'No, indeed I assure you I sent my little cousin no note. I would not dream of addressing her except through you, when you have been placed in charge of her by her mother. I have been considering, indeed – I intended to telephone you today and ask you to call ... Some proper provision must be made, of course. But I did not ... This is terrible! You do not think that someone has lured her away ... ? But who knew of her presence here? Your friends of the film unit, you tell me, are in Benares. Otherwise who could know you – and Anjli – here in Delhi, and know where to find you?'

'We've been in contact with a lot of people in the town, of course,' admitted Tossa, 'but only casually, the sort of tourist contact one has with shops, and restaurants, and guides ... and what could be more anonymous? The only place where we're *known*, so to speak, apart from here and the hotel, is the house in Rabindar Nagar – your cousin Satyavan's house ...'

'Of course!' Dominic snapped his fingers joyfully. 'Why didn't I think of it! Kishan Singh! A slightly grubby little note brought by a paid messenger ... It could be! Kishan Singh may have had some news of Anjli's father. Perhaps he's home!'

Vasudev looked first dubious, and then hopeful; and after a few seconds of thought, both excited and resolute. He came out of his western chair in a nervous leap. 'Come, we shall take the car and I will drive you over there to Rabindar Nagar. We must see if this is the case. Indeed, one hopes! That would resolve all our problems most fortunately.'

He ran to the rear door of the palatial hall, and clapped his hands, and in a few moments they heard him issuing clipped, high-pitched orders. Presently the car rolled majestically round on to the rosy gravel, with a magnificently turbaned Sikh at the wheel. A glossy new Mercedes in the most conservative of dark greys, and its chauffeur's pride and joy, that was clear by the condescending forbearance with which he opened the door to allow them to enter its sacred confines. But that morning he was not to be allowed to drive it; Vasudev did that himself, and did it with a ferocity and fire they had not expected from him. Their taxi driver, on the first occasion, had taken half as long again to get them to Rabindar Nagar.

At the first turning into the new suburb from the main road Vasudev braked, hesitating. 'It is long since I was here, I have forgotten. Is it this turn?'

'The second one. N block, it's only a couple of hundred yards farther on. Yes, here.'

At the half-finished houses the bold, gypsyish, stately women of Orissa walked the scaffolding with shallow baskets of bricks on their heads, and made a highly-coloured frieze against the pale blue sky, their fluted skirts swaying as though to music. At sight of the opulent car the half-naked children padded barefoot across the open from their low, dark tents, running beside it with pinkish-brown palms upturned and small, husky voices grating their endless complaint against possessing nothing among so many and such solid possessions. There was no obsequious tone in this begging, it accused, demanded and mocked, expecting nothing, and ready to throw stones if nothing was given. But this time the plump lady from next door did not chase them away. She was there, she and a dozen others, clustered round the open iron gate of N 305, all shrilling and shrugging in excited Hindi, a soprano descant to a louder, angrier, more violent clamour of male voices eddying from within the compound. No one had time now for errant children; the centre of all attention was there within the wall, out of sight. And even the Orissan infants, having come to beg, sensed that there was more to be had here than new pice, and winding the excitement, wormed their way in under elbows, between legs, through the folds of saris, to see whatever was there to be seen.

'Oh, God, no!' prayed Tossa silently in the back seat, tugging at the handle of the door. Little girls vanished, little girls reappeared, horribly changed. Everybody knew it happened. But not here! With all its violence and despair and hunger, somehow India had felt morally clean and safe to her, she would have walked through Old Delhi at night, alone, and never felt a qualm, something she couldn't have said for Paddington. Yet unmistakably this had the look of a crowd round the police van, the ambulance, the sorry panoply of murder or rape.

The clambered out of the car, clumsy with haste.

'Oh, dear! Oh. dear!' Vasudev keened, his voice soaring with agitation. 'Something has happened! Something is wrong here! Miss Barber, you should please stay in the car...'

But she was already ahead of them, boring into the small butterfly crowd about the gate, and thrusting her way through without ceremony. They followed her perforce, clinging to her arm, urging her to go back. Tossa hardly noticed. It was bad enough for them, but it was she who had taken on the job, so lightly so selfishly, coveting India and hardly thinking, at first, about the child who was being posted about the world like a parcel...

She extricated herself frantically from the gold-embroidered end of a lilac and white sari, and fell out into the open space of the compound, and Dominic flung his arm round her and held her upright. The door of Satyavan's house stood wide open, and on the white paving before it Kishan Singh, his guileless eyes round and golden with fright, sobbed and protested and argued in loud Hindi, alternately buffeted and shaken between two vociferous Punjabis in khaki shorts and tunics. Another man in khaki, obviously their superior, stood straddle-legged before the trio, barking abrupt questions at the terrified boy, and swinging a short rattan cane of office in one hand. He was a handsome turbaned Sikh, his beard cradled in a fine black net, his moustache waxed fiercely erect at the ends. Whatever had happened, the Delhi police were in possession here.

Kishan Singh, turning his bullet head wildly from one persecutor to the other, caught a fleeting glimpse of the new arrivals, and uttered a shrill cry of relief and joy. Crises in India are chaotic, voluble and exceedingly noisy, and he had been adding his share to this one, but only out of panic. With someone to speak for him, he regained his sturdy mountain calm.

'Sahib, memsahib, please, there is very bad thing happened. You tell these men, I am honest, I have done nothing wrong... Why should I call police here, if I did this thing?'

Dominic looked squarely at the Sikh officer, who was plainly the man to be reckoned with here. 'Kishan Singh is the caretaker of this house, and has been a good servant to Shrimati Purnima Kumar and to her son. If Shrimati Purnima were still alive, I know she would speak for her boy, and I feel sure Mr Kumar here, her nephew, will tell you the same. I don't know what has happened here, but I know that Kishan Singh is to be trusted.' Did he really know that, after one short encounter? Yes, he did, and he wasn't going to apologise for the brevity of the acquaintance to this man or to anyone. With some people, you know where you stand, with some you don't. Kishan Singh belonged among the former group. There is an innocence which is absolute, and there's no mistaking it when you do meet it.

'I understand,' said the Sikh officer, eyeing them narrowly, 'that this boy is the only resident here. Is that the case?' His English was all the better because his voice was a sombre bass-baritone.

'Yes, I understand that is true. Apart from the old man who lives in the compound here, as a kind of pensioner of the family.'

'Ah ... yes,' said the police officer gently. 'That is the point. We are, unfortunately, debarred from referring to this elderly gentleman as a witness.'

'I know he is blind. You mean there has been a crime on these premises?'

'A very serious crime.' He made a brief gesture with the cane in his hand, and deflected all attention into the distant corner of the compound, partially cut off from view by the jut of the house wall. Tossa wanted to close her eyes, but did not; what right had she to refrain from seeing what was there to be seen? The poor little girl, shuttlecock to this marital pair who didn't care a toss about her, and now fallen victim to some incomprehensible perversion that was an offence against India as well as against youth and girl-hood . . .

'Come, you should look more closely,' said the Sikh, and led the way, turning once to say with authority: 'The lady must stay here.'

The lady stayed; she could not very well do anything else. But her eyes, which had excellent vision, followed them remorselessly across the sparkling white paving, across the beaten, rust-coloured earth, under the lightly-dancing clothes-line, to the shed and the lean-to roof in the corner, where Anjli . . .

No! There was no honeyed rose of Anjli's skin there, and no midnight-black of her hair, and no silvery angora pink of her best jersey suit. There were two policemen and one dried-up little medical civilian sitting on their heels around something on the ground; and when the Sikh brought his accidental witnesses over to view the find, these three rose and drew apart, leaving the focus of all attention full in view.

He could not have been found there, any chance passer-by in the side street might have looked over the wall and seen him; they must have brought him out into the light after measuring and recording his position on discovery, somewhere there in the corner shed, fast hidden from sight.

The dull brown blanket was gone. Only a thin, skinny little shape, hardly larger than a monkey, lay contorted on the darker brown earth of Satyavan's yard, bony arms curled together as if holding a secret, bony legs drawn up to his chin, streaky grey hair spread abroad like scattered ash. There was so little blood in him that his face was scarcely congested at all; but there were swollen bruises on the long, skinny, misshapen throat to show that he had died by strangulation.

The eyes were open; blank, rounded and white as pearls.

Arjun Baba, that very, very old man, had quitted the world in the night, and left no message behind him.

Kishan Singh padded across the yard at the policeman's heels, protesting: 'I did not touch the old man, I swear it. Sahib, why should I touch him? All this year I have given him food, and brought him his *pan*, and been as his servant, as my mistress told me. Always when I rose in the morning he was sitting by his brazier... Today he was not there. I called him, and he did not answer, and therefore I looked within... Sahib, he was lying there in the dark, as you see him, so he was. I saw that he was dead... Also I saw how he had died, and therefore I ran for the police. Should I do that if I had killed him?'

'It would be the best way of appearing blameless,' said the Sikh officer drily, 'if you had the wit.'

'But why should I wish to harm him, I? What gain for me? You think such a person had money to be stolen?'

'You may have grudged the effort of feeding him. Perhaps he was in your way. It would be easy to make away with some of the furnishings of this house, without a witness always in the compound...'

'The old man was blind...'

'But very quick of hearing,' called the plump lady from next door, bright with excitement at the gate; and all the neighbours joined in in shrill Hindi, shouting one another down. 'Everything he heard! I had only to set foot on my roof, and he would call up to me. He knew by my walk when I had my washing basket on my arm.'

'This boy has been always a very trustworthy servant,' Vasudev urged in agitation. 'I cannot believe he would hurt the old man.'

'You do not know what he might do, being master here as well as servant. Young people have no time now to care for the old ... Arjun Baba was a trouble to him, that is how it was! Who else was here to do this thing, tell us that? In the night we are not minding our neighbours' business here, we are good people. Very easy to make away with the old man in the night, and then find him – oh, yes, all innocently! – in the morning and run to the police.'

Other voices rose as vociferously, arguing against her. The two policemen, affronted by the steady surge of curious people across the threshold into the front garden, began to push them back outside the gate, were shrilled at indignantly in consequence, and shouted back no less angrily. The noise soared into a crescendo that was like physical pain. And all the while Dominic and Tossa gazed at the shrunken, indifferent corpse of Arjun Baba, old age torn and savaged and discarded where they had dreaded to see Anjli's youth and grace. It is a terrible thing to feel only relief when you are brought face to face with a murdered man. They felt themselves, in some obscure way, responsible, if not for his death, yet for the absence of all mourning; if the world had not owed him a living, yet surely it owed him at least justice and regret now that he was dead.

'If you did not do it, then who did? Who else would want to kill such an old man? Who were Arjun Baba's enemies?'

'He had no enemies ... No friends now except me ... and no enemies ... I do not know who would do such a thing. But I did not ... I did not ...'

89

In the fine drift of dust along the lee of the old man's hut a tiny gleam of whiteness showed. Dominic stepped carefully past the stringy brown feet, and stooped to pick up the small alien thing no one else had yet noticed. It lay coiled in his palm light as a feather, seven inches or so of fine green cord stringing a bracelet of white jasmine buds, threaded pointing alternately this way and that. After sixteen hours they were a little soiled and faded, one or two torn away from their places, but they were still fragrant. He saw that the green cord was not untied, but broken; and silk is very strong.

Anjli had been here!

He began to see, vaguely, the shape of disturbing things. Anjli had been here, and the flowers she had worn had been ripped from her wrist with some violence, perhaps in a struggle. And the old man, the only one remaining who had been here when Satyavan vanished in the night, was dead. Anjli had given him a token, and coaxed him to tell her whatever he knew. And last night Anjli had received a grubby note brought by a common messenger, a note which had sent her out secretly before dawn. To this place. For so the jasmine flowers said clearly.

He turned to the Sikh police officer, shouting to make himself heard. 'Have your men examined all Arjun Baba's belongings? May I know what you found?'

'Belongings? Sahib, such a man has nothing ... a brazier, a headcloth, a loincloth, a blanket ...'

'But you see he *hasn't* got a blanket! And it was a cold night!'

It was true. The policeman cast one swift glance into the hut, and frowned, and looked again at Dominic, who was becoming interesting. With more respect he enumerated one by one the few poor items of Arjun Baba's housekeeping.

'Nothing more? Not even a tiny thing like a gold coin?'

A shrug and an indulgent smile. 'Where should such a man get gold?'

Had the token been sent back, then, as bait to bring

Anjli? And if so, by whom? By Arjun Baba in good faith? Or by his killer? A missing gold dollar to lure her to the meeting in the dark, a missing blanket to muffle her cries and smother her struggles ...

'I'll tell you,' he said, 'where he got gold. From a young girl who came here with us a few days ago, and gave him the dollar she wears on a chain for luck. We came here looking for her, and I really think we'd better tell you the whole story, because it looks as if she has been here in the night, and whoever killed Arjun Baba has also taken Anjli away. Can't we go into the house, where it will be quieter? This may take some time.'

It would have taken less time than it did if someone could have restrained Vasudev's slightly hysterical commentary of pious horror and masochistic self-reproach. Wasn't he, perhaps, protesting even a shade too much? Tossa's thumbs were pricking painfully before the whole story was told. True, Vasudev had willingly brought them here, and in a hurry, too, but might not that be part of a carefully-laid plan? The anxious relative, conscious-stricken over his own shortcomings towards his young cousin ... who was going to look there for a murderer and kidnapper? There was a lot of Kumar money, and this dutiful managing director of all that wealth had got into the habit of thinking in millions by now. Who could wonder if...? Some people would even have difficulty in blaming him!

'It would seem,' said the Sikh policeman, summing up with a good deal of shrewdness, 'that this young lady is the child not merely of one very wealthy person, but of two almost equally subject to envy. If, as you say, she has indeed been kidnapped, the motive must be gain. There is almost no other known motive for kidnapping, unless the object is matrimony. For love, of course! One understands that gain may also be involved in matrimony, but that is by the way. Then the first question that arises is: how many people, here in India, knew that Miss Kumar is worth much money as ransom? All of the members of this film company, that is certain. Most are Indians, they would know that the Kumar family are millionaires. The others, the Americans, even if they were not so well informed about the Kumars, would know that the mother is famous and rich.'

'They'd know more than that,' said Dominic bluntly. 'American film actresses don't usually marry poor Indians.'

'That is well observed. Money, Mr Felse, is inclined always to money, there is an affinity. So we have all the film company. And who besides? Your household, Mr Kumar, I think could hardly be ignorant of the young lady's value, after her visit to Mrs Kumar's death-bed. News is very quick to travel among servants, and you have many servants. Then also, let us not forget, this house-boy here, Kishan Singh, is not an idiot, and Miss Kumar had expressly revealed her identity to him...'

'After I had already done so,' said Dominic stoutly. Whatever happened, he could not imagine circumstances in which he would suspect Kishan Singh.

'Very naturally. The fact remains, he was, by your account, the first after the film company to know of Miss Kumar's value. But when we have said that, let us not be misled, we have not closed the number of our suspects. Film stars are news. For all we know there may have been paragraphs in the papers about Miss Kumar's arrival in India. It would need only one observant person on the same flight. And once here, interested eyes may have observed your visit to Mrs Kumar's villa. Also here.'

'That lets nearly everybody in,' admitted Dominic glumly.

'Nevertheless, those with close personal knowledge – priority knowledge, one could say – must take precedence. Leave it to us, we shall investigate every person concerned. There remains the possibility that Miss Kumar is at liberty, and for her own reasons in hiding. This we can surely confide to you, Mr Kumar. Miss Kumar, I understand, is not familiar with Hindi. But a personal advertisement in the

92

English-language press would be, I suggest, a good idea?
She may very well read the papers! She will be unable to
resist looking to see what they say about her!'

Vasudev seized on it as on a lifeline in a very rough sea.
Practicalities were his line. He was out of his chair in an
ecstasy of enthusiasm, looking at his watch.

'I shall see to it at once. There is the evening press . . . if
you will pardon me, it would not be too late . . . But my
guests . . . is it possible to arrange transport wherever they
may wish . . .? Or perhaps I could return a little later . . .?'

'It's quite all right, thank you very much,' said Tossa.
'There's a taxi rank just on the main road.'

'Then if you will excuse me . . . ! Please do get in touch if
you should have any news, and naturally I will do the same.
Your servant, Miss Barber!'

He had a small leather-bound notebook in his left hand
as he galloped out of the room, and a ball-pen in his right,
so anxious was he to get his come-home-all-is-forgiven advertisement framed for the evening papers. And it might be
genuine, and it might not, and who could hope to tell the
difference? The Sikh officer, perhaps. He stood at the window, frowning down towards the dusty frontage, until the
Mercedes had started up and rushed away with aplomb in
the direction of the main Delhi road. But by the sombre
look on his face as he turned back into the room, he had
come to no very definite conclusion about Vasudev. Nor,
perhaps, about them? After all, if Anjli was a prize, who
knew her worth better than they did, and who had been in a
better position to manipulate her movements?

'Now, Mr Felse, a few more questions.' They turned out
to be more than a few. Had he, had Tossa, ever previously
been in contact with any of the Kumar family? What did
they know of them? It was clear why Vasudev had been
sidetracked out of the picture for the moment. Patiently
they went over and over their very brief acquaintance with
the Kumars, withholding nothing.

Had they had any undisclosed communication with Kishan Singh? They did realise that even if some other person

with more sophisticated ideas conceived the plan of kidnapping Anjli and holding her to ransom, yet Kishan Singh
was the obvious tool to use?

'He's the last tool *I* should use,' said Dominic with conviction, 'for anything dirty.'

'An innocent face may be a gift from God even to the
unworthy. But we were not – or did I not make that too
clear? – speaking necessarily of *you*. Kishan Singh may
even have conceived the plan himself after witnessing – you
did say he witnessed it? – the scene between the young lady
and the old man. How easy to send her the symbol and ask
her to come here! About that I am sure you are right. She
may, as it were, have originated the whole plot herself in
that impulsive act.'

And had they anything to add to their account? Any
forgotten detail? Dominic, by this time, had remembered
that he had not mentioned hearing, or thinking he heard,
Ashok's morning raga whistled the previous night in the
courtyard of Keen's Hotel, at the very time when the note
was being delivered to Anjli; but he had seen enough of the
way the land lay to keep that item to himself now. The
issue was confused enough already, why introduce into it
what he might well have imagined, and what would certainly smell like a red herring to this suspicious person
interrogating him?

'Very well, let us leave it at that for the moment. You
will be available, please, at Keen's Hotel, you will not move
from Delhi at present.'

'We are not going anywhere,' said Dominic steadily,
'until Anjli is found. And I hope you are not thinking of
detaining Kishan Singh, because he, too, will be available
whenever you need him. He won't leave here unless the
Kumar family tell him to, and a word from you will take
care of that.'

'You are very concerned for the house-boy, Mr Felse. It
is generous on your part – and interesting.'

'I am concerned because he is young, alone here – his
mistress, as you must know, is recently dead, and his family

94

in the hills – and quite certainly totally innocent. You have only to look at him. He has never in his life entertained a malicious thought, much less deliberately hurt anyone. Arjun Baba was as sacred to him as the sparrows that fly in and out of the house. The boy was responsible for him to Mrs Kumar, whom he revered absolutely . . .'

'And who, as you have pointed out, is dead. One person's death may bring about a total disintegration for her dependents . . .'

They were raising their voices, both of them, and that made Tossa aware, quite suddenly, in what low tones they had been conversing for several minutes past. She pricked up her ears, and leaned upon a wall of noise that was not there, and fell through it into full consciousness. The din from the yard, that flat, clattering chaos of voices one gets used to in India, aggravated here by excitement to a sustained pandemonium, had almost completely ceased. When, she had no idea. Simply, it was gone. She reared her head, straining after it, and recaptured only a gentle, single murmur, unbelievably placid and reassuring.

'Listen!' she said peremptorily; and in sheer surprise they fell silent, too. 'It's gone quiet. What's happened?'

The wonderful hush fell on them and charmed them into stillness. And stillness and silence, in Delhi, represent a new and more menacing crisis. The Sikh officer wheeled and strode to the window, with Dominic and Tossa pressing discreetly on his heels. They stared down into the yard together, forgetting all disagreements; for in their own way they were all the forces of law, and law had not sufficed to bring about silence and stillness in the confines of N 305, Rabindar Nagar, in the teeth of suspicion and disorder.

Drawn up in front of the gate stood an extraordinary car. Only a Rolls-Royce, perhaps, could have driven up so quietly as to be unnoticed. It was certainly an extremely antique Rolls-Royce, not at all well-maintained as far as its noble chassis was concerned, though apparently mechanically in first-class condition. Orissan children swarmed about it with absorption and delight, and were fended off

95

good-humouredly, when necessary, by a long, slender, crop-haired driver in khaki shorts and bush jacket, who lounged at ease on the running-board. The women at the gate had stopped yelling, and stood decorously in a staged group, expressive of grief and modesty and respect, all facing inwards towards where Arjun Baba's little wasted corpse lay uncomplainingly exposed. Beside the body stood a personage as remarkable, in his unassuming way, as his car, and for all his venerable appearance no more than half as old again. Put the man down as rising sixty, the car as around forty, and you wouldn't be far out. Neither showed its age except in non-essentials. It was perhaps incipient baldness which had induced the man to shave his subtle and exquisitely-shaped crown, and climatic, seasonal rust which had suggested the removal of the world-famous radiator cap, and the substitution of a small brass knob from a bedstead; but both were spry, agile, in full working order, and would take some catching when in the mood.

The man was not even tall; he didn't have to stoop to lay an arm about Kishan Singh's shoulders, and Kishan Singh was squat and square. Nevertheless, the impression of lofty height was there, dominating everyone within sight. It may have been the erect and aloof carriage, it may have been the slight withdrawal of the naked, golden, ascetic head on its slender neck, the poised effect of a stylised bronze which withdrew him into the field of art. It certainly was not innocent, but equally certainly it was not posed. He knew what he was, and employed it fully for his own inscrutable ends; and what mattered was what dictated the ends. He had a gentle bronze face, thin of feature and disarming of expression, live dark eyes moving modestly within the sculptured head, fleshless bones as serene as weathered mountains, and a benevolent smile like the antique stone smile of Angkor, at once calming and shattering. He wore a robe of saffron cloth that fell in chiselled folds to his ankles, and over it a knitted shawl draping his shoulders. His feet looked like bronze skeleton feet in the worn leather sandals. He had his arm round Kishan Singh's

96

shoulders; the aura of his protection encompassed the boy in an almost visible glory. The two policemen hovering in the fringes of his influence looked now like attendant figures in a religious picture.

What was most humbling of all, the dominant figure sensed the presence of the watchers at the window above, within a minute of their gathering there, and with a gesture of his hand most courteously invited them to descend and rejoin the tableau.

Which, for want of a more appropriate response, they forthwith did.

VII

'You must forgive us,' said the newcomer, 'for so inopportune an arrival. We had no idea that we should be intruding upon a problem and a tragedy. My name is Premanathanand. I am one of the members of the Native Indian Agricultural Missions, and I came here today to visit the home of my old friend Satyavan Kumar. I have been away on field studies among our settlements until recently, and for some time have had no opportunity of seeing him, and it is a friendship I value. But these ladies tell me – and the house-boy here – a good boy, I knew him in Mrs Kumar's household in Kangra – that Mr Kumar is not here at present. Also that there is a matter of the young girl, his daughter, who has vanished from the care of her guardians.' That, of course, must have come from Kishan Singh, who had been the only one of these people close enough to overhear what had passed between Dominic and the police officer before they went into the house, and who would tell everything without reserve to a man he trusted. In which case, Dominic thought, he would also have told him that Satyavan had been gone more than a year, and no one, not even his own mother, had known where he was, and no one knew now. That made this already interesting person even more interesting, since he had glided so gently over Satyavan's absence, as though he had merely gone away for the weekend.

And it was, now that he came to study it at close quarters and somewhat below the level of his own, an extraordinarily ambiguous face, at once candid and withdrawn, giving and reserving, just as his smile both comforted and disquieted. Every detail you looked at was as ordinary as the dusty soil of Delhi; the saffron robe, if you observed it closely, was worn, a little faded, and frayed at the hem, the brown

98

knitted shawl round his shoulders had a stitch worn through here and there; his hands were sinewy and broad-jointed and used to hard work; the spectacles on his thin, straight nose were steel-rimmed and had battered wire ear-pieces, and one lens was thicker than the other, so that they tended to sit askew, and the eye seen through the thick lens was startlingly magnified. Yet the sum of the parts was so much more than the whole that accurate observation was disarmed. His voice, mild, clear and low, held the same ambivalence as his appearance; its serenity had a calming effect, but it left disturbing echoes behind in the mind, like the still, small voice of conscience.

'It is not for me,' he said courteously, smiling at the police officer, 'to ask questions in what must seem no affair of mine. Though as a friend of the child's father, I cannot but be concerned for her safety.'

And, perhaps it was not for him to ask, but he had made it clear that he would like to be told, and the Sikh officer told him. The large-lidded, intelligent brown eyes proceeded from one face to another, acknowledging the characters in the drama, smiling benignly upon Tossa and Dominic, brooding impassively over the small dead body now covered with a white sheet from the sun and the stares.

'It would seem,' he said at length, 'that someone who knew of Miss Kumar's gift and request to Arjun Baba conceived the idea of making use of that incident to lure her here, so that she might be abducted. It was necessary to the scheme that Arjun Baba should be removed both to get possession of the token, and also so that someone else could take his place, and wait here for the girl. It seems, therefore – do you not agree? – that though we have here two crimes, we have but one criminal.'

'That is my conclusion also, Swami,' said the Sikh respectfully.

'It would therefore be well, would it not, to concentrate on solving the crime which affords the best possibility, first, of salvaging something from the harm intended, and, second, of affording a sporting chance of arresting the

99

criminal.' His varied and surprising vocabulary he used with the lingual dexterity of a publicist, but with the absent serenity of one conversing with himself. 'Arjun Baba here is dead and cannot be saved. But the girl is alive and must be kept alive to be worth money, and therefore she can be saved if we are circumspect. And upon the second count – he who killed Arjun Baba has now no interest but to remove himself from here and hide himself utterly. But he who has taken the child *must make overtures*, in order to gain by his act, which was his whole object in taking her. Therefore he must make the first approach, and in making it may reveal himself.'

'Exactly, Swami. And therefore it is clear that we must concentrate on the kidnapping of the girl, and we shall thereby also find our murderer.'

'You are excellently lucid, Inspector,' said the Swami with admiration and relief. 'You make everything clear to me. You would conclude also, if I follow you correctly, that since the father is not here and knows nothing of this crime, there are now two possibilities: either the criminal knows where to find him, and will approach him directly; or he does not know, and will therefore approach the equally plutocratic mother. Or, of course, her representatives.' His benign but unequal gaze dwelt upon Tossa and Dominic, and returned guilelessly to the Sikh Inspector of Police. 'I am glad that so serious a case has fallen into the hands of such an intelligent officer. If there should be any way in which I can help, call upon me. You know where our Delhi office is situated?'

'I know, Swami. Everyone knows.'

'Good! Whatever I can do for Satyavan and his daughter I will do. And this boy may be left in charge of this house? It would be well, and I will vouch for him, that he will be here whenever you wish to question him...'

'I had no thought of removing him from his trust, Swami.' And that might be true, or might be a gesture of compliance towards this respected and remarkable man; but Kishan Singh would welcome it, whatever its motive.

'Then I shall leave you to your labours. Ah, yes, there is one thing more. Arjun Baba has neither wife nor sons. When you release his body for the funeral rites, I beg you will give it into my charge.'

'Swami, it shall be done as you wish.'

The Swami's mild brown eyes lingered thoughtfully upon Tossa and Dominic. 'I am sorry,' he said civilly, 'that you have suffered such a troubled introduction to this country of ours. If you are now returning to Delhi, may I offer you transport? There is plenty of room, if you do not mind sharing the back of the car with some grain samples we are carrying. And I should like, if you have time, to offer you coffee at the mission.'

'Thank you,' said Dominic, stunned into compliance like everyone else in sight, 'we should be very grateful.'

The policemen, the women at the gate, even the Orissan bandit babes, fell into a sort of hypnotised guard of honour as the Swami Premanathanand walked mildly out of the compound of N 305, Rabindar Nagar, with the two English strangers at his heels. The long, languid driver rolled himself up nimbly from the running-board and opened the rear door for the guests, but no one was looking either at him or at them, all eyes were on the Swami. He had, perhaps, the gift of attracting attention when he chose, and diverting it when he chose. At the moment it suited him to be seen; perhaps in order that other things should pass unseen. He took his seat beside the impassive driver. The small grain sacks in the back were piled on the floor, and hardly embarrassed even the feet of the passengers. The Rolls, especially in its ancient forms, is made for living in. With pomp and circumstance they drove away, almost noiselessly, from the scene – they all thought of it now first and foremost as that – of Arjun Baba's death.

Anjli Kumar, quite certainly, was still alive to be salvaged.

The Delhi headquarters of the Native Indian Agricultural Mission lay in Old Delhi, not far from the crowded

precincts of the Sadar Bazaar. They had half-expected a
gracious three-acre enclosure somewhere in a quiet part,
with green lawns and shady buildings; instead, the car
wound and butted its way between the goats and tongas and
bicycles and children of the thronging back streets, and into
a small, crowded yard surrounded by crude but solid
wooden huts. In a minute, bare office two young men con-
ferred over a table covered with papers, and at the other
end of the table a girl in shalwar and kameez typed
furiously on an ancient, spidery machine that stood a foot
high from the board. All three looked up briefly and smiled,
and then went on passionately with what they were doing.
In an inner room, creamy-white, a brass coffee-table and
folding canvas chairs provided accommodation for guests,
and a cushioned bench against the wall offered room for the
hosts to sit cross-legged. A litter of pamphlets and newspapers lay on the table, and all the rest of the walls were
hidden behind bookshelves overflowing with books.

The girl from the typewriter brought coffee when she
had finished her page, and the Swami sat, European-style,
round the table with them. And presently the driver came
in silently and seated himself Indian-fashion at the end of
the bench, respectfully withdrawn but completely at his
ease, drinking his coffee from a clean but cracked mug, and
watching the group round the table with intelligent black
eyes and restrained but unconcealed curiosity. He had shed
his sandals on the threshold; his slim brown feet tucked
themselves under him supply, and the hands upturned in
his lap, nursing the mug of coffee, were large and sensitive
and strong. The Swami did not hesitate to refer to him
when he wanted another opinion, or confirmation of a recol-
lection.

'Girish will recall when last Satyavan visited me here. It
is surely more than a year.'

'It was in September of last year,' Girish confirmed. His
voice was quiet and low-pitched, and his English clear as
his master's. Unsmilingly he watched the Swami's face.

'I do not wish, of course, to take your responsibility from

102

you. It was to you that the child was confided, and you best know her mother's mind. You have told the police all that you can, and now you will consider, I know, what more you must do. But if you have anything to ask of me, at any time, I am here. We have a telephone, write down the number, and call me whenever you will.'

By that time he knew where they were to be found in Delhi, and all about them, even to the one thing they had not told the police. He sat mildly smiling, or even more mildly grave, and they told him things they had hardly realised they were thinking.

'But that's too fanciful,' Tossa said doubtfully. 'Dominic is musical, but I can't believe he could simply recognise Raga Aheer Bhairab when he heard it . . . not after a single hearing.'

'But that's the whole point,' Dominic objected warmly. 'I never claimed I recognised Raga Aheer Bhairab, what I recognised was a straightforward folktune, a song Ashok himself said had to reach everybody at first hearing. And the more I think about it, the more I'm sure that's just what it did. I bet somebody who had heard the Brahms Wiegenlied only once would know it again the next time.'

'However, as you tell me, this film unit is now in Benares. And this man, the director . . .?'

'Mr Felder,' said Dominic.

'He is, you say, an old friend of the girl's mother, the friend to whom she turned when she wished someone to meet you on arrival. You would say that he has her confidence?'

'Yes, I'm sure he has.'

'In the absence of both parents, he might, perhaps, be the best adviser? But you will consider what you ought to do, and do it, and it is not for me to meddle. If I can provide any helpful information, I shall get in touch with you. And if you receive news of the child, I beg you will let me hear it, too.'

They thanked him and promised.

'Girish will drive you back to your hotel.'

103

Dominic sat beside the taciturn chauffeur on the journey back to Keen's, and studied the profile beside him curiously out of the corner of his eye. A hawk-like Punjabi profile, high-nosed, clear of line, with a proud, full, imperious mouth, and cheeks hollow beneath bold, jutting bones. When he smiled all his features flashed into brightness; but he smiled only once, when Tossa asked diffidently exactly what the Swami was, monk, priest, Brahmin or what.

'The Swami is himself, what else can one say? He does not conform to any prescribed order, and he does not recognise caste. He does not do what is expected of him, or even what is required of him – he is too busy doing what he wants to do and what has to be done. I doubt if any group would dare to claim him – or care to own him,' he added, more surprisingly.

'And what does this Agricultural Mission of his do?'

'Whatever it can to improve stock – but *that's* an uphill struggle! – or bring in better methods of farming and cultivating. Through village co-operatives, small voluntary irrigation works, improved seed, local dairying schemes, new cropping methods – anything, wherever we can find the right material for the work. We try to make such village co-operatives self-supporting, and even self-reproducing. To be clear of debt is to attract envy. To show a profit is to stimulate imitation. We have some foundling farms, too, where the children who are left to fend for themselves by begging can do a small share of the work and get a fair share of the food. Even a seven-year-old is useful for some jobs.'

'Seven ...!' Tossa drew breath incredulously. 'But surely such young children ... You mean you *get* them as young as that? Just drifting in, *on their own*?'

'On their own,' he agreed. The ancient Rolls turned majestically into the drive of Keen's Hotel. 'In our country, too,' said Girish levelly, staring ahead between the high hedges, 'there are neglected and forsaken children.'

They argued it out between them over a lunch for which

neither of them had any appetite, and came to a decision. Even if they had not been gently prompted by the Swami they would probably have come to the same conclusion.

'Even with the police in on it,' said Dominic, summing up, 'we've still got to face our own responsibility. We simply have to let someone know what's happened. Kumar's out of reach, and Dorette – let's face it, what good would it be telephoning Dorette? All we'd get – all Anjli would get – would be hysterics. Dorette wouldn't come out here to take charge herself, not with a film half-finished, and that's the sober truth. And even if she did, she'd be no use at all. But there's Felder. *She* turned to him when she needed somebody here, in a way he's a sort of representative of Dorette. And he's sensible, and knows his way about here. If he says we must call Dorette, then we'll do it. But let's at least consult him first.'

So he telephoned Clark's hotel at Benares, and by luck the unit happened to be in for lunch. The sound of Felder's vigorous voice over the line was cheering, and the promptness of his decisions bracing.

'Now look, you hold it right there, and I'll be with you as soon as I can. We haven't finished shooting, but this is an emergency, and they'll just have to get along without me. There's an afternoon flight, if I can get a seat on it. Don't worry, the airlines office is right here in the hotel. You stay close to home, in case there are any messages, and I'll come straight to you there.'

'Messages?' Dominic repeated, thinking hopefully of the police calling to tell him Anjli was already traced, and as good as found.

'Well, they can't get at *him*, if no one knows where he is, can they? And you're the nearest available channel to Dorrie, aren't you?'

Air travel comes into its own in India, where you can transport yourself at very reasonable cost from Calcutta to Gauhati, or Trivandrum to Madras, or even from Delhi to Srinagar across a minor range of the Himalayas, in roughly the time it takes to go from Birmingham to London by train. Thus it happened that Ernest Felder, having bluffed and persuaded his way into the last available seat on the afternoon plane from Benares, was in Keen's Hotel by seven in the evening, his grey hair on end, his lined, easy-going face for once desperately grave. Over dinner, which by that time they all needed, he got them to tell him the whole story all over again, in detail, and with as much detachment as was possible in the circumstances. He didn't exclaim, he didn't swear, he simply listened with every nerve, helped out with a question here and there, and soothed them by the very fact of his large, zestful, intent presence and the degree of his concentration. If sheer compact energy could recover Anjli, she was as good as saved.

'Now, let's not get tangled with non-essentials. The facts are, someone went to a lot of trouble to get Dorrie's girl. And there's no reason on earth why such an elaborate plot should be laid to get her into the right place, except just plain money. Somebody knows her value. There's a rupee millionaire of a father, and a film star mother. There's money, and plenty of it. Right?'

They could not but agree.

'So they now have to get in touch with all that money, in order to tap off as much of it as the traffic will stand. Right? And as we've said, the father is out of the picture ... *unless* the kidnappers know more than we do. If they know how to get in touch with him, so much the better, that will bring him into the open, and we can all join forces. But if they don't they're going to be after Dorrie. But my guess would be, not directly. There are complications once you start sending messages of that kind across frontiers, from here to Europe – even if they know where to find her, and my guess is they may not, though pretty obviously they must know who and what she is. No, they'll make their play in the safest and nearest direction. And that's *you*! You represent Dorrie here, you're Anjli's temporary guardians. My bet is that you can expect instructions from whoever's got Anjli, and pretty soon.'

106

'Supposing there's any choice,' said Dominic firmly, 'we can't risk Anjli.'

'No, I agree. Any instruction they give must be obeyed absolutely. We can't take any chances with Dorrie's kid. I wouldn't with anybody's kid, for that matter. What about this Cousin Vasudev you were talking about? You reckon they're likely to contact him? ... as kind of a tap for the family money? Family is a great thing here, they might well figure he'd pay out for her, supposing he has legal access now to the funds. Company or family. I don't know how they're fixed.'

Tossa and Dominic didn't know, either. Their voices took on a certain reserve when they spoke of Cousin Vasudev.

'Sure, I know! He stands to gain. But he could be on the level, too. And if he isn't, it won't do any harm to shake him up now and again, he might give something away. But whoever took the little girl knew all about that gold dollar, that's what gets me. And this cousin of hers didn't – or at least not from you, not until today ...'

'But he could have from Kishan Singh,' Tossa pointed out. 'We told him we'd come straight from there, he might very well question the house-boy afterwards; and Kishan Singh would tell a Kumar everything. From his point of view, why not?'

'That's true, that's very true. Maybe a neighbour, even, could have overheard when she gave it to the old man. I don't know, I just don't know! All our bunch may have known all about it, from that time you telephoned for me and got Ashok, and gave him the whole story to hand on to me ... but then, most of the bunch are away in Sarnath still, and have been since early the morning after you called, before Anjli was snatched.'

Dominic had laid down his fork with careful quietness. *'Most?'* He met the blank, enquiring stare, and elaborated uneasily: 'I thought you *all* were.'

'Well, all the working unit, yes, and nearly all the players. Not Kamala, of course – Yashodhara doesn't appear in the Deer Park scenes. This is where the sacred brotherhood line begins. No women on the scene for a while.'

'I see.' Dominic reflected that he should have taken time off, like Anjli, to read the book, and he might have been somewhat wiser in his assumptions. All the women left behind in Delhi! He thought for a moment, and asked without undue emphasis: 'And Ashok?'

'Ashok? In India you don't ask an artist of that calibre to run around after you, *you* run after *him*. We show the rushes for Ashok, right here in Delhi, and he broods over them three or four times, and comes up with the music for the sound-track when he's good and ready. Oh, yes, he likes to spend a good deal of time with us down at Hauz Khas, but that's a bonus. He enjoys us. But not enough to go blundering about in Sarnath with us on the day's grind.'

'I see,' said Dominic again, making more readjustments. But this picture of Ashok, on the face of it, removed him still farther from any possibility of participation in a sordid crime for gain. 'I suppose he must be in the film star class himself, then?'

'Just about. I know what you're thinking of – this tune you heard the chap in the garden here whistling – but you don't even know that it was the chap who brought the note, do you? And for goodness sake, some of the sweepers and drivers around the villas and the office could have heard Ashok playing that theme and picked it up. He meant it to be catchy. And believe me, he isn't satisfied with one run through when he's recording, not to mention all the practising beforehand. I shouldn't worry too much about that. Even if you're right about it!' And plainly he was by no means convinced about that, and on the whole Dominic could hardly blame him. Nobody else had been convinced, either, not even Tossa.

'Mind if I hang around with you this evening? Just in case anything happens?'

'I wish you would!'

'I shouldn't have any peace if I left you to it,' said Felder

108

almost apologetically.

They adjourned to Dominic's sitting-room, and waited the evening through; and no one got much rest, when it came to the point. The strain of waiting for something to happen is not conducive to conversation, and presently even monosyllables faded out. Eight o'clock passed, and nothing broke the tension. Nine o'clock, and still nothing. Half-past nine . . .

Felder shook his solid shoulders and sighed. 'Nothing's going to happen tonight, it seems. I wonder if they went for Vasudev and family loyalty, after all?'

And it was then that the telephone rang.

All three of them started wildly, as if a gun had been fired; all three of them came to their feet, staring at the instrument, even reaching out for it, half afraid to take the plunge. Dominic looked up over the white handset at Felder.

'Yes,' said Felder rapidly, 'you take it. Hold it till I open the door, then answer it, and if it *is* – give me the sign, and I'll slip down to the switchboard and see if it can be traced. And – *listen!* – *if* it is, talk back, hold him as long as you can, give us a chance. *And don't miss a word he says!*'

He took a couple of quick strides backwards and opened the door of the room. Dominic lifted the receiver.

'Hullo . . . Dominic Felse here.'

'You are the gentleman who has lost some valuables,' said a high, strident, clacking voice in his ear. 'I have them, they can be recovered.'

Dominic's mouth was suddenly so dry that for a minute he could not make any answer. He nodded strenuously at Felder across the room, and the big man slid noiselessly through the door he was holding open, and drew it to after him, releasing the latch slowly so that it made not a sound. In the telephone the voice crackled impatiently: 'I know you hear me. You want your lost property back. I can provide. Of course at a proper price.' An old voice, he thought, or at least elderly; its tone cracked when it was raised, it had no body in it, and no juice. On first hearing, either male or female; but he thought, male. He moistened his lips feverishly, and instinctively began to waste time.

'Who is that? Are you sure you're on the right number? This is Felse speaking, you wanted me?'

'It is you who want me, my friend,' said the voice, and cackled painfully in his eardrum. 'If you want Miss Kumar, that is.'

'How do I know you really have any information about Miss Kumar? Where are you speaking from? Who are you? How do you know anything about it?'

'That is very well put, how do I know! How could I know, except that *I have her*? Oh, she is safe, quite safe. You want proof? Miss Kumar has American passport...' Horrifyingly the old voice rattled off its number, the place of its issuing, the personal details of her description, and giggled unnervingly at the blank silence that ensued. 'You can have this lady back for two hundred thousand rupees – cash.'

'But that's impossible ... you must allow us time, at least, how can we command cash at short notice...?' Dominic protested, feeling round the apparently empty recesses of his mind for any prevarication he could find, anything to keep the man talking; while at the same time he struggled to record every word that was said. 'I don't believe you have her. You could have found her handbag, or stolen it, and got hold of the passport that way. If she's there, let her speak to me, and I'll believe...'

The voice cut him off sharply. 'Listen, if you want her! You get that two hundred thousand rupees, you get it in mixed notes and put it into a cheap black school bag. And on Sunday afternoon at two o'clock...'

'Sunday?' gasped Dominic in utter dismay. 'But that's only two days! How can we...'

'... on Sunday, I say, you go, you and the woman also, to the Birla Temple. You leave your shoes with the lame boy who sits at the foot of the steps, on the right, and with your shoes the case with the money. Then you go into the temple

110

and stay within for half an hour, not one minute less. Do not try to keep watch on your shoes, do not say one word to the police, or anyone else, if you want to see the girl again. Put on your shoes and go back to your hotel. On Sunday evening I call you again and we arrange about the child. *If* you have done as you are told.'

'But, listen, we want to co-operate, but it's a question of time, damn it! – You must give us longer than that ...'

'Sunday. If you want her.' The line echoed one quavering ring, and was dead. Dominic held the receiver numbly for a moment, and then very gently cradled it. His knees gave under him, and he sat down abruptly. 'My God, it's impossible, we *can't*! I don't believe it can be done, not by cable, not even by telephone.'

'Why?' Tossa urged, pale and quiet. 'What did he say? What is it he wants?'

'Two hundred thousand rupees by Sunday. *Sunday!* Now we've *got* to call Dorette Lester, we've got no choice. But I doubt if we can get the money through by then, whatever we do ... whatever *she* does!'

'We *have* to. There has to be a way. I don't even know,' she said helplessly, 'how much two hundred thousand rupees is. It sounds a fortune.'

They were still gazing at each other, stunned into silence, when the door opened, and Felder came into the room. Both tense faces turned upon him, though without much hope. He shook his head glumly.

'A call box, somewhere central, that's all we had time to get. Probably on Connaught Circus. One step out of the box, and he'd be a drop in the ocean. Not a chance of getting anything on him. What did he have to say?'

Dominic cleared his dry throat and told them, practically word for word. It wasn't the sort of message he was in any danger of forgetting.

'He didn't give anything away ... about himself? What did he sound like? I suppose,' he added, struck by a sudden doubt, 'it *was* a he?'

'I think so. Yes, I'm sure. But at first I did wonder ... a

111

high-pitched, thin voice ... old ... No, he didn't give a thing away. And now,' said Dominic, 'there's nothing for it but to tell Miss Lester, and hope she can cable the money in time... But, damn it, *Sunday*! It won't be a banking day here. We've only got tomorrow.'

'There's Vasudev,' ventured Tossa dubiously. After all, they had harboured doubts about Vasudev's cousinly solicitude. All that money, old Mrs Kumar newly dead, Satyavan, by his own design or another's, utterly vanished, and only this little girl between Vasudev, the dutiful manager and nephew, and all those millions of rupees and that commercial empire. Even if he hadn't got her out of the way himself, what a temptation this might be to want her kept out of the way now, to hinder, not help, any attempt to pay the ransom and recover her alive.

'And besides,' said Dominic flatly, as if he had followed her unspoken thoughts thus far, 'we've been warned, not a word to any outsider. Maybe they haven't realised that we've got Mr Felder in on the job already, but I bet they wouldn't miss it if we went near Vasudev between now and Sunday afternoon. And we daren't take any risks with Anjli.'

'It won't be necessary, anyhow,' said Felder slowly. He sat down heavily, and his big shoulders in their immaculate tailoring sagged back into the chair as if he had suddenly grown very tired. 'It won't be necessary to frighten Dorrie yet, either ... if all goes well, it need never be necessary, only in retrospect. We'll put up the money, and we'll make sure of being on time with it. As you say, we can't take any risks with Anjli.'

They were watching him with wonder, and as yet carefully suppressing the hope that he knew how to work miracles, and could make his word good now.

'No, *I* haven't got that sort of money here, don't look at me like that. *I* haven't, but the company has. We've got a big credit in the bank here to cover this Buddha film. And it so happens that it will run to two hundred thousand without being sucked dry, and when necessary my signature is

112

enough to draw on it. If I left anything undone that I could do for Anjli, I'd never be able to look Dorrie in the eye again. And she'll replace the loan as soon as she knows the facts. Tomorrow I must draw the money out of our bank, and you can buy a cheap school briefcase, just as he said, and we make the payment. *You* make the payment, rather – and *I* stay out of sight and keep an eye on your shoes.'

The wild flush of relief came back to Tossa's face, and the brightness to her eyes. Dominic let out a long, grateful breath.

'Oh, *lord*, if we *could*! Is it really all right for us to borrow it? But you wouldn't try anything then, would you? I mean, we agreed we had to obey instructions, for Anjli's sake.'

'I would not! But I'd have a shot at trailing whoever takes the briefcase, that's for certain. Once we get Anjli back, I'm all for putting the police on to her kidnappers.'

'But is it going to be possible to hang around and watch the place, like that? Won't you be too noticeable?'

'You haven't seen the Lakshminarayan temple on a Sunday afternoon! It's like a fun-fair. Cover galore and thousands of people. Might make it hard for me to keep an eye on him, but it will certainly reduce his chances of spotting me. It's worth a try, at any rate.'

'The Birla temple, he said,' Dominic pointed out.

'Same thing, laddie. Lakshminarayan is its dedication, and the Birla family built it. They had to do something with some of the money, it was getting to be a bore.' There was a faint snap of bitterness in this lighter tone; no wonder, when they had need of a comparatively modest sum at this moment for so urgent a reason, and were put to such shifts to acquire it.

'I can't tell you,' Dominic said fervently, 'how grateful we are for your help.'

'Not a word, my boy! I've known Dorrie for years, and didn't she ask me to keep a fatherly eye on you over here? But I tell you what, I'd better get out of here by the garden way tonight, hadn't I, and keep away from you except where we can be strictly private?'

He rose and stretched wearily. There were times when he looked an elderly man, but always withindoors and in presence of few if any observers.

'Is there nothing I can be doing?' Dominic asked anxiously, aware of having ceded his responsibilities to a degree he found at once galling and reassuring.

'Sure there is. You can go out in the morning – maybe alone would be best, if Miss Barber doesn't mind? – and buy a cheap, black, child's briefcase. Somewhere round Connaught Place there are sure to be plenty of them. And about half past ten you could oblige me by being inside the State Bank of India, the one in Parliament Street. If you're seen going in there, that can only be a good sign. And I'll come separately, they won't know me. And we'll take out that two hundred thousand rupees – that's something over eleven thousand pounds, I'd say offhand. You know, that's not so exhorbitant, when you come to think about it! – and see it packed up all ready for the pay-off, and packed into that briefcase. And in a couple of days we'll have Anjli out of bondage.'

VIII

On Saturday morning they drew out the money from the film company's account in the State Bank of India in Parliament Street. Dominic was there waiting with his plastic school briefcase in his hand before Felder arrived; in good time to admire the imposing appearance his colleague made after a night's rest and a careful toilet, immaculate in dark grey worsted. The clerk treated the whole transaction as superbly normal, and was deferential to the point of obsequiousness, perhaps because of the size of the withdrawal. Felder was carrying a much more presentable brief-case in pale chrome leather; Dominic had never seen him look the complete city sophisticate before. Even his tone as he asked for the money to be made up in mixed notes was so casual and abstracted that any other course would have seemed eccentric.

So that was that. They were moving at leisure away from the counter, with two hundred thousand rupees in assorted denominations in a large, sealed bank envelope, linen-grained, biscuit-coloured and very official-looking. It seemed like having a hold on Anjli again. Suddenly it seemed an age since Dominic had seen her face or heard her voice, and he remembered the jasmine flowers, with the strange ache of an old association fallen just short of love.

'Put it in the case now,' suggested Felder in a low voice, proffering the crisp new parcel before they were in view from the doorway. 'Or would you rather I locked it in the office safe until the time comes?'

'Yes, you keep it. Drop it off at the desk for us tomorrow, there'll be plenty of people in and out. Supposing there is someone watching me now, he may think it a good idea to knock off this lot before I can get it back to the hotel, and then ask for more. How can I be sure?'

'All right, as you like.' Felder shrugged his shoulders ruefully. 'I suppose it is my responsibility.' The envelope disappeared into the chrome leather case, swallowed from sight with a magnificent casualness. Briefcases of that quality went in and out of here by the score, black plastic scholastic ones were much rarer in this temple of commerce. Dominic felt grateful that he had bought Everyman copies of the Hindu sciptures and the Ramayana and Mahabharata, to give a semblance of gravity to his own flimsy burden. They could easily have been mistaken for money, viewed from the outside.

'In the morning, then, about ten, I'll bring it to the desk. Better be somewhere close, in case. And when you leave the temple in the afternoon, come in to Nirula's for tea. I'll be there.'

'We will,' said Dominic.

'Go ahead first, then, I'll give you ten minutes or so.'

Dominic walked briskly out of the imposing doors of the State Bank of India, and away down Parliament Street, with his tawdry briefcase filled and fulfilled with the wisdom of thirty centuries of Indian thought and feeling. Worth a good deal more, in the final issue, than two hundred thousand rupees, even taking into consideration the relative impossibility of adequate translation.

It was the longest Saturday they ever remembered, and the only good things left about it were that they had at least a hope of recovering Anjli, and that they were spending the agonising time of waiting together. Felder kept away from them, and that was surely the right thing to do. And they made contact with no one, so that if they were watched the watchers might be quite certain that they had not infringed their orders. They went no farther from their hotel than the Lodi park, where they sat in the sunshine among the fawn-coloured grass and the flowers, the amazing, exuberant, proliferating flowers of the season, and looked at the towering rose-coloured tombs with which the Lodi dynasty had burdened the Delhi earth, and thought about Purnima's

116

modest pyre by the Yamuna, and her little heap of ashes
going back to the elements, and nothing left of weight or
self-importance or regret. And it seemed to them the most
modest of all ways of leaving this world, and the most in
keeping with the spirit's certainty of return; until, of
course, the cycles close in the last perfect circle, and you are
free from any more rebirths.

But they did not stay away long, because they were afraid
of being out of reach, even by ten minutes' walk, in case
there was some new message. They had very little sleep
that night. Felder, in the smaller villa at Hauz Khas, fared
no better. All of them were up with the first light, and
aching for the afternoon to come.

To reach the Shri Lakshminarayan temple, if you happen to be in the shopping centre of Delhi, Connaught Place,
you strike out due west along Lady Hardinge Road, and it
will bring you, after a walk of about a mile, straight to that
amazing frontage. Don't expect anything historic; the
temple was built towards the end of British rule, as a
gesture towards the wholeness of all the Indian religions,
which are still one religion, so that it belongs to orthodox
Brahmans, Sikhs, Jains, Buddhists, and anyone else, in fact,
who comes with sympathy and an open mind. It is dedi-
cated to Narayan and Lakshmi, his spouse, but it also
houses images of others of the Hindu pantheon. Which
pantheon is itself an illusion, a convenient veil drawn over
the face of the single and universal unity; convenient, because its multifarious aspects provide an approachable deity
for everyone who comes, from the simplest to the most
subtle, and from the most extrovert to the most introvert,
and all routes that lead to the universal essence are right
routes.

What Dominic and Tossa saw, as they turned into the
final straight stretch of the road and emerged into the broad
open space of Mandir Marg, facing the forecourt of the
temple, was a huge, gay, sparkling construction in several
horizontal terraces, above a sweeping flight of steps, and

117

crowned above by a triple shikhara, three tall, fluted, tapering towers, shirred in a pattern imitative of reed thatching, each capped at its sealed crest by a yellow cupola and a tiny gilded spire. The towers were mainly white, picked out with yellow, the levels below them were white and russet red and yellow, lined out here and there with green, arcades of mannered arches and perforated balustrades. All the textures, all the colours, were matt and gauche and new; and with their usual assured recognition of realities, the modern inhabitants of Delhi had taken the place for their own. Felder had not exaggered. It was a fairground; a happy, holiday, Sunday-afternoon crowd possessed it inside and out.

Mandir Marg was teeming with people and traffic. They crossed it warily, Dominic hugging the cheap little briefcase that contained the bank's envelope full of money, which Felder had left at the desk at Keen's that morning.

There was plenty of space for all who came, about the front of the temple. But approximately half of that space was cordoned off behind frayed white ropes, sealing off the actual front of the temple wall beside the staircase. Within this enclosure stood and sat half a dozen or more vociferous Hindus, jealously guarding serried rows of footgear discarded here by the faithful, and waiting patiently for their return. Just to the right of the steps sat a diminutive brown boy, slender and large-eyed, one thin leg tucked under him, one, clearly helpless and distorted at the ankle, stretched out like a purposeless encumbrance at an improbable angle. A home-carved crutch lay beside him. He had more than his fair share of sandals and shoes to mind.

Tossa and Dominic shook off their sensible slip-ons, and proffered them tentatively across the cords. There is always the problem of tipping now or when you recover your property. The uninitiated prefer to play safe by doing both, even if this involves over-paying. Dominic gave the boy a quarter-rupee, reserving the other quarter for when they emerged, and held out the briefcase to be placed with their shoes. The child – how old could he possibly be? Thirteen?

118

– seemed to be content. Even conscientious, for he lined up the two pairs of shoes with careful accuracy, and stood the briefcase upright between them. And yet he must be in on this thing... Or was that necessarily so? There could be somebody he knew and trusted, a credible story, a planned diversion ... No, better withhold judgement.

They climbed the steps. Delhi receded and declined behind them. Through the arcaded doorways sweet, heady scents wafted over them, sandalwood, incense and flowers, an overwhelming, dewy splendour of flowers. This is the season of flowers in Delhi; the marvellous shrubs and trees blossom a little later. But the sense of approaching a fair-ground remained. Why not? Fairs are essentially religious in origin, and if they are joyful occasions, so should religion be.

They stepped into spacious halls faced everywhere in parti-coloured stone and polished marbles, brightly lighted, swarming with curious, reverent, talkative people, notably hordes of alert, lively, fascinated children. Formalised gods sat brooding immovably under mini-mountains of flowers, little bells chimed ingratiatingly, reminding the remote dreamers that small, insistent worshippers were here re-questing attention. Everything was fresh, naive, festive and confident; religion and everyday life knew of no possible barrier or even distinction between them. The fragrance was hypnotic; there was a kind of radiant dew upon the air. And yet if you cared to be hypercritical you could fault everything in sight as garish, crude and phoney; you would be mistaken, but in that mood you would never recognise the fact.

The pale, sharp sunshine fell away behind them, and the delicate blue fingers of perfumed smoke brushed their faces. They had been told not to watch their shoes, and not to emerge again for half an hour exactly. They obeyed instructions to the letter.

Felder stood on the opposite pavement, watching the ceaseless flow of people about the steps of the temple, the play of coloured saris and the flutter of gauze scarves. A man alone could stroll this length of street on a Sunday afternoon for as along as he would, and it was highly improbable that anyone would notice him among so many. From time to time he moved along to a new position, drew back into the shade of the frontages for a while, crossed the street to mingle with the crowd over there in the sun, and even climbed the steps and wandered along the open terrace; but seldom, and only for seconds, did he take his eyes from the little black case propped upright between the two pairs of shoes. At the far end he descended again to the street and made his way back along the edge of the roped enclosure, among the darting children and the idling parents, and the hawkers selling glass bracelets, spices coloured like jewels, bizarre sweetmeats and heady garlands. Half an hour can seem an eternity.

No one had approached the lame boy's corner, except to hand over more shoes to be guarded. The briefcase lay close to the rope, within reach of a hand, and the boy was busy; it would not be impossible to snatch the thing and vanish with it among the crowd. But there it stood, demurely leaning against Dominics's shoe, a small black punctuation mark in a pyrotechnical paragraph.

A quarter of an hour gone, and nothing whatever happening. He turned to retrace his steps once again, and cannoned into a wiry fellow in khaki drill trousers and shirt and a hand-knitted brown pullover in coarse wool. The man was bare-headed and clean-shaven, his complexion the deep bronze of an outdoor worker; and by the way he recoiled hastily and obsequiously from the slight collision, with apologetic bobbings of his head, Felder judged that he was not a native of Delhi. When Felder, for some reason he could not explain, turned his head again to take another look at him, the fellow was still standing hesitant on the edge of the pavement, looking after the man he had brushed. He looked slightly lost among this confident crowd, and slightly puzzled, as if he had somehow come to the wrong place.

120

Felder put the man out of his mind, and concentrated again upon the black briefcase. But eight minutes later, when he came back that way, the man was still there, and this time the thin face with its strongly marked features and large dark eyes turned towards him with clear intent.

'Sahib, I beg pardon,' he said low and hesitantly in English. 'Can you please help me? I am stranger here. I am not from Delhi, I come from the hills. Please, this is Birla Temple?'

'Yes, that's right.' He had no wish to stop and talk, but it would be difficult to withdraw from this unsought encounter too ruthlessly, for supposing there was more in it than met the eye? Supposing someone had become suspicious, and was keeping him under observation, as he was keeping watch on the briefcase?

'And, sahib, is here also Birla House? I wish to see Birla House.' In the gardens of that princely residence the Mahatma was shot and killed; but it lies a matter of two miles away from the Lakshminarayan temple. Felder supposed it was possible that a simple hillman sightseeing in Delhi might expect to find the two in close proximity.

'No, that's quite some way from here. You could get a bus, I expect, it's well south, close to Claridge's Hotel.' Absurd, he thought the moment he had said it, as if this chap from out of town would be likely to know Claridge's.

'Sahib, I have no money for bus.' Clearly he was not asking for any, either, it was a perfectly simple statement. 'I will walk, if you can show way.'

Felder had to turn his back on the temple for that, and point his pupil first directly away from it, down Lady Hardinge Road towards Connaught Place. 'Take the third turning on the right into Market Street, and go straight on down to the parliament building. You've seen it?'

'*Acha*, sahib, that I have seen.'

'Then you cross directly over the Rajpath, and keep straight ahead down Hastings Road, and at the end of Hastings Road you'll find Birla House occupying the corner of the block facing you.' Accustomed to the visual imagination, Felder demonstrated the direction of the roads in the air, an invisible sketch-map. The dark eyes followed it solemnly, and apparently with understanding.

'Sahib, you are most kind. I am grateful.' Large, lean, handsome hands touched gravely beneath the hillman's chin. He bowed himself backwards towards Lady Hardinge Road, and then turned and walked purposefully away.

Felder heaved a breath of relief, watching him go. It was all right, after all, the man was genuine, and had had no interest in him but as a source of information. He turned quickly, and his eyes sought at once for the small black speck close to the lame boy's side, sharp and sinister against the pale tawny ground. The interlude had not caused him to miss anything, it seemed.

The half-hour was over, and Dominic and Tossa were just emerging into the blinding sunlight from the fragrant dimness of the temple. And the black briefcase was still there.

In the quietest corner of Nirula's they gathered over the tea Felder had already ordered before the other two arrived. They had no heart for it, but he poured it, just the same. They were going to need every comfort, even the simplest.

'But what went wrong?' Tossa was asking, of herself no less than of them, and with tears in her eyes. 'We did everything he said, we didn't tell anyone else – they *can't* have known about *you*! – and we didn't say a word to the police – and you don't know how unlikely that is, until you know Dominic, his father's a police inspector, and all his instincts bend him their way, they really do! And yet we *did* play it the way we were told, and we were in good faith, though it's horrible to submit to an injustice like that . . . And yet at the end of it all, here it still is, not touched, and we're no nearer getting Anjli back!'

The briefcase lay on the cushioned bench-seat between them, plump and weighty as when they had surrendered it to the lame boy.

'We just couldn't believe it, Mr Felder! What are we

122

going to do now? And what made them hold off? They can't have known about you, *can they*? Could they possibly have spotted you hanging around, and called the whole thing off?' She was ashamed of the suggestion as soon as she had made it, after all he had done for them. 'No ... I'm sorry, don't listen to me!'

'I don't believe anyone did notice me,' Felder assured her gently. 'All the more because I did once wonder ... but it turned out quite innocently. No, I just don't believe it.' His eyes lingered speculatively on the briefcase, smugly filled and flaunting its roundness. He frowned suddenly, regarding it. In quite a different tone, carefully muted so as to arouse no extravagant hopes, he said: 'Open it! Go ahead, let's be sure. Open it.'

Dominic stared and bridled, and then as abruptly flushed and obeyed. They were jumping to conclusions; they hadn't even looked. He pushed a thumbnail fiercely under the press fastener that held the case closed – how flimsy, and how quickly sprung! – and drew out the identical biscuit-coloured bank envelope they had placed there, still sealed as it came from the bank, nearly four hours ago. He stared at it with chagrin; so did they all. Then abruptly Felder uttered a small, smothered sound of protest, and took up the packet, turning it in his hands. He ran his fingers under the transparent tape that sealed the flap, and wrenched it open. Out into his lap slid a tightly-packed wad of sliced news-print. He ran the edges through his fingers, and the soft, close-grained, heavy segments mocked them all. There was not a banknote in the whole package, nothing but shredded newspaper.

'My *God*!' said Felder in a whisper. 'After all! Then he *must* have been planted ... No, I can't believe it, they never had time!'

'It wouldn't,' said Dominic slowly, 'take very long. A fastener like that is a gift. But only if you had another packet ready to substitute. If they watched me go into the bank yesterday ... But could you possibly guess at the bulk of it so closely? I suppose the bank envelope wouldn't be

123

any difficulty. But *could you*? And was there any time when it could possibly have happened?'

'You could,' said Felder, with soft, intense bitterness, 'if there was enough at stake, I suppose. And yes ... there was maybe two and a half to three minutes. I'd swear it wasn't longer. There was this countryman from somewhere in the hills ... I had the feeling he might have been planted on me, but when he went away so promptly ...' He told them, baldly and briefly. 'It couldn't have been more than three minutes in all, that I'll swear. As soon as I told him, he went. He never even looked back. I'd know him again, that's for sure! But God knows where he is now! And yet he sounded genuine, and when I told him his way he was off like a hare.'

'Does it matter?' said Tossa suddenly. Her eyes were bright and hopeful. 'Maybe we didn't pin him down, whoever he is, but does it matter so much, after all? The money's been collected. It wouldn't take much ingenuity to get hold of a large bank envelope, would it, once they'd seen Dominic go in there yesterday morning? But what matters is, the ransom's been collected, after all. They've got what they asked for. They promised us a call this evening, if we played by their rules. They promised us a call "to arrange about the child". They've got what they wanted, why shouldn't they let us have her back now? They're safer that way, and they've scored a success, haven't they?'

She was right there was no doubt of that. Maybe they had failed on one count, but it was a failure that might very well net them a total success on the main issue.

And the main issue was, and always would be, Anjli.

They waited all the evening in Dominic's sitting-room at Keen's, whither Felder had repaired via the garden staircase and the balcony. Eight o'clock went by, nine o'clock, half past nine ... The telephone remained obstinately silent.

But at a quarter to ten there was a sudden insinuating rapping on the door. Dominic sprang to open it, even though this was not at all what they had expected.

124

Into the room, serenely calm as ever, and beatifically smiling, walked the Swami Premanathanand. Down below in the courtyard the ancient Rolls stood with folded wings and reposeful outline, like a grounded dove.

IX

'I trust you will forgive,' said the Swami courteously, 'so late and unceremonious a call.' He looked from Dominic to Felder, whom he had never seen before, and his wise brown eyes, behind the unequal lenses, refuged deep in the shadow of large ivory eyelids and kept their own counsel. He even seemed able to suppress the unnerving magnifying power of the strong lens when he chose. 'I am afraid that I have interrupted a private conference. But you will understand that I am exercised in my mind about Mr Kumar's daughter. I may speak freely?'

'Yes, certainly,' said Dominic, torn several ways at once and quite incapable of resolving the struggle. 'This is Mr Felder, who is an old and valued friend of Anjli's mother. Mr Felder is directing a film here in India, and he has been very kind to us since we came. And this is the Swami Premanathanand, of the Native Indian Agricultural Missions, who is an old friend of Mr Kumar.'

'Delighted!' said Felder feelingly. 'We can certainly use another friend here ... and another good sound head, too. If I'm right in taking it that the Swami knows what's going on?'

'I have that honour,' said the Swami shyly, and modestly accepted the chair Dominic offered. Tonight he wore an old European trench coat, minus the belt, over his saffron robe, and when he stripped it off in the warmed room his one shoulder emerged naked and polished and adamant as bronze, bone and sinew without the more dispensable elements of flesh.

'You have received no trustworthy news about Anjli's whereabouts?'

'No,' said Tossa miserably, 'But we *have* had a telephone call to say she's being held to ransom.' She could see no reason at all for concealing anything that had happened; passionately she recounted the events of the afternoon. 'And we're no farther forward at all, and they're not going to keep their bargain. We've been waiting here all the evening for a telephone call, and *nothing*! They've cheated us. And now we haven't any way at all of getting in touch with them, it was a one-way traffic. We've just poured that money down the drain, and it wasn't even ours, it has to be replaced. And I can't bear to think...'

'If money has been demanded and taken,' said the Swami, smoothly interrupting the downward cadence of her grief and self-blame, 'then clearly money is the means to further negotiation. This first sum was very easily come by, there is a strong temptation to repeat the success. Do you not agree, Mr Felder? You are a man of the world, where money counts for more, perhaps, than we realise who want it only to invest in crops and food and development. The actual notes we scarcely even see. Nevertheless, they exist, and there are those who know how to value them. And there are those who have them, and know how to devalue them when there is something of great worth to be bought.'

'I'd give whatever I could raise,' said Felder warmly, 'to get Anjli back. But I've shot not only my own bolt, but the company's too. Right now I'm bankrupt. If Dorrie stands by me, I'll pull out of it. If she doesn't, I'm sunk. And what did I buy for her? Not a thing!'

'You have done what you could. It is now for others, perhaps with greater responsibility, to do as much as you have done. Also it is for them to appreciate at its true worth the thing which you have done.' Benevolently the great eye, like a rare and awe-inspiring omen, beamed through the pebble-thick lens, and again was veiled as his head turned. Like the lance of light from a light-house its brief, comprehensive flash encompassed them all, and withdrew itself into dimness. He raised a lean, long-fingered hand, and took off his glasses. Mild, short-sighted eyes, one brighter than the other, blinked kindly at Dominic. 'Since I saw you I have been active ceaselessly upon one problem, that of

127

where Satyavan Kumar might be found. I have sat beside the telephone and pondered the possibilities, testing all I considered valid. There are universities where he has studied, colleges where he has lectured, laboratories where he has taken part in research. There are the ordinary places where he directed, not always willingly, the business of his family's interests. But there are also places to which he withdrew sometimes for refreshment of the spirit, ashrams, solitudes, hermitages... And some of these I have, in the past, shared with him.' He looked up obliquely, smiling with the delicate pleasure of a child bringing gifts, but a child acquainted, in some obscure amalgam of innocence and experience, with maturity and age. 'I have run up,' he said, with the sprightly nonchalance that emerged so surprisingly from his normally measured and precise vocabulary, 'the very devil of a telephone bill. But *I have located Satyavan.*'

'You *have*?' Dominic shot out of his chair joyfully. This couldn't be the whole answer, it couldn't solve everything, and above all it couldn't absolve Tossa and himself, but the surge of relief and release he felt was wonderful. The father should have been there from the beginning, he should never have let go, at any cost, of that fragile essence of himself that survived in Anjli. He shouldn't have given up what was his; and he must know it, in this extreme, better than anyone. If he was found, they had an elemental force on their side, a tornado that would sweep away obstacles like a breeze winnowing chaff. 'Where *was* he, all this time? What's he been *doing*?'

'Is he coming?' demanded Tossa, slicing straight through to essentials.

'Where he has been I cannot tell you, surely in many places. Where I found him was in a place of the spirit where we have sometimes rested together when there was need. One does not ask too many questions of those one meets there, for only the answer to one question is of any importance, and that is; from here, whither? And yes, he is coming. There will be a plane from Madras arriving tomorrow a little after noon.'

'Then he didn't know,' said Tossa, quivering, 'that his mother was dead? He didn't see the newspapers?'

'He did not know until it was too late ... no. One does not always read newspapers. There is a time *not* to read them, if you wish to remain upright.'

'Then you had to tell him?' she said, her eyes, dark and luminous with sympathy, fixed on the austere old face that confronted her with such serenity. 'That must have been very hard for you both. And then, his child...'

'It is never easy,' said the Swami apocryphally, 'to return to the world. Until you have left it, you cannot know how hard. But there is no other way forward and none back. Yes, I told him all that it was necessary to tell. And to-morrow in the afternoon he will be here.'

'But what can he do?' demanded Felder. 'God knows I shall be glad to have him emerge into the light again, and get hold of his responsibilities. He's taken his time about it! But it's the kid we're concerned about, and how is he better placed than we are to get her back? Damn it, we did what they told us to do, we paid what they asked for, and they're ratting on the deal. What more has he to offer, when it comes to the point?'

'About twelve million rupees more,' said the Swami Premanathanand with all the aplomb and all the cold blood of a banker or a saint. And he added patiently, as to un-realistic children: 'Do not forget we are concerned with people whose requirement is essentially simple ... money. That puts us in a very strong position, because Satyavan is in command of a very great deal of money – now, as you know, in almost complete command of it – and to him it means very little. It sweats from his finger-ends, money. Daughters are infinitely harder to come by. He will pay whatever is necessary to recover Anjli. He has told me so with his own lips. To the limit of what he has, he will pay for her.'

'But how,' wondered Tossa distractedly, 'do we get in touch with them? They can reach us, but we don't know how to reach them.'

'That probably won't be a problem,' Dominic said bitterly, 'as soon as her father emerges. After all, they must be watching absolutely any developments in connection with the family, they wouldn't miss a thing like that.'

'You may well be right. But in fact Satyavan has left as little as possible to chance. I have here the text of a personal advertisement which I have composed at his dictation.' He felt in the deep pocket of the trench coat, which was draped like a cloak of office over the back of his chair, and produced a folded sheet of paper. 'It is his wish that this shall appear in tomorrow's newspapers ... all the main ones – in the personal column. It is too late to get it into the morning press, but we are in time for the evening papers. If we are not successful with this approach, then of course it may be necessary to let the newsmen have some item to use concerning the return of Mr Kumar, but for the moment he judged it better to come home as quietly as possible and attempt a private contact.' He unfolded the sheet of paper, and perched his spectacles back upon his long, narrow, beautiful nose. 'This is how it reads: "Anjli: Am interested in your merchandise. High price if delivered in good condition. Full guarantees." Then I had intended to give Mr Kumar's home number and request a call at a fixed hour any evening – hoping, of course, that it will come tomorrow evening if the advertisement has been seen. But if you would permit, I think it would be better now to say only: "Call usual number, eight p.m. Kumar." If you will allow this telephone to be used as before, I think it might avoid alarming the vendors.'

Felder uttered a soft whistle of admiration. 'You think of everything!'

'If one must do such things at all, it is necessary to think of everything. And therefore I cannot any longer avoid,' said the Swami mildly, 'pointing out to you the one remaining possibility with which, unfortunately, we also have to count. Though it may well be that you have thought of it for yourselves, even if you have refrained from expressing

130

it. Anjli may already have been killed.'

Tossa nodded wretchedly, Dominic stood frozen eye to
eye with the fear he had hoped she need not share, and
Felder protested aloud, all in the same instant.

'Good God, no! They surely wouldn't hurt the child.
I'm sure she must be alive and safe somewhere.'

'It is common practice in cases of kidnapping. Such
people tend to make certain that they can never be identi-
fied, and the obvious witness is the victim.'

It was doubly terrible to hear this said in that tranquil,
matter-of-fact voice. Felder looked grey with shock and a
little sick; but still he shook his head vigorously, resisting
the foreboding. 'No, it's impossible. I'm certain she's alive
and well.'

'Let us hope so. But the criminals have not kept their
bargain with you. There must be a reason why you have not
received the expected call. Either it is a further gesture of
greed to hold on to her for still more money, since the first
demand was so encouragingly successful. Or else they cannot produce her, and you will hear nothing more. Her
father's arrival will resolve that problem. For I must tell
you that he will insist on seeing with his own eyes that his
daughter is unharmed, before he even enters into negotia-
tions. What is more, on my advice he insisted that you, who
may now know her more certainly than he himself would,
shall also see her and verify that it is indeed Anjli. He has
not set eyes on her for six years, a substitute might be
passed off on him if you were not present to confirm her
identity.'

'But how,' asked Dominic with patent dismay, 'can we
hope to make them agree to taking a risk like that?'

'That is for them to arrange as best they can. Satyavan
will agree to any safeguards they suggest, provided he can
satisfy himself that there still exists something to be
bought. If they want their money – and it will be worth
their while – they will go to some trouble to arrange it.' He
added: 'I also have promised that the police will not be
drawn into the affair by me, though of course, as you know,

131

they are already informed about the crime itself. A quick settlement is therefore much to the criminal's advantage.'

'I hate,' said Dominic with sudden and uncharacteristic passion, 'to think of them getting away with it.' And it came out as a plain protest against the Swami's apparent acceptance of the possibility. True enough, the main thing was to recover Anjli alive and well, and restore her to her rediscovered father. But even so, the ugliest and meanest of crimes ... not to speak of Arjun Baba's thin but tenacious thread of life, snapped almost by the way ...

The Swami rose, faintly smiling, and put on his trench coat. 'I am more fortunate than you in this respect, that my beliefs assure me that no one ever *gets away* with anything. There is a constant account which must balance. In what form of life these people will return to earth it is useless to conjecture.'

'Cockroaches, probably,' said Tossa with detestation, and saw Felder wince perceptibly. In India cockroaches are the nightmare of the uninitiated.

'Ah, cockroaches are sagacious and relatively harmless creatures! Do not attribute human malice to them. And now I shall leave you,' said the Swami, 'until tomorrow evening. If you agree that I may bring my friend here to hope for his daughter's return?'

'Yes, please do! None of us can rest until we get her back.'

Only after he had withdrawn did it occur to Tossa, to her amazement and shame, that they had not offered him any refreshment in return for his typist's excellent coffee. The magnetism of his presence was such that one sat at his feet while he was in the room. And yet, when it came to the point, what did they really know about him?

Felder went out on to the balcony outside the window, and looked down into the courtyard, curious about the ancient Rolls with its tattered body and indestructible heart. The driver had just observed the Swami approaching from the garden entrance of the hotel, and slid nimbly out from behind the wheel to open the door for his master.

132

'Wouldn't you know he'd have that sort of car? I bet everything he does and everything that belongs to him measures up. Say what you like about this country, at least it has a sense of *style*.'

Tossa and Dominic came to his side and stood looking down with him as the Swami clambered majestically but athletically into the lofty front passenger seat, which had something of the throne about it. As Girish closed the door a large taxi came prowling into the patio from the drive, and its headlights focussed directly upon the Rolls. Girish moved at leisure round to the driving seat, head raised to free his vision from the momentary glare. Felder uttered a sudden sharp moan of astonishment, and leaned out far over the balustrade.

'Oh, *no*! It can't be . . .!'

'Can't be what? What's the matter?' Dominic asked in alarm.

'That fellow . . . Look! The driver . . .' At that moment the headlights swerved from Girish, and left him to climb into the Rolls in shadowy obscurity, and so start up his noble vehicle and drive it away.

'Girish? What about him? He's the Swami's regular one . . . at least, he's the same man who was driving him when we first met him.'

'He's the hillman who stopped me outside the temple this afternoon,' Felder said with certainty, 'and asked me the way to Birla House. That's who he is! The guy who took my attention off the pay-off briefcase just long enough to get the contents swopped over.'

'*Girish?* But he . . . damn it, he drove us home . . . Are you *sure*?'

'I'm sure! I'd know that face again anywhere. Now you tell me,' said Felder savagely, 'why a man who can drive his boss about Delhi smartly enough to be worth his pay should have to ask his way to Birla House? Go ahead, tell me! I'm listening.'

After which, it was hardly surprising that a conveniently

133

anonymous taxi, with three people aboard besides the driver, should sit waiting for the arrival of the plane from Madras, at something after noon the next day at Safdarjung Airport. The passengers didn't care to venture out on to the tarmac, because the ancient Rolls was there in all its glory, with Girish lounging at the wheel, and the Swami Premanathanand had gone briskly through the airport buildings to the landing frontage, to wait for the emerging travellers. Instead, the taxi parked in a convenient position to watch the new arrivals proceeding towards their town transport. The Sikh driver, efficient, intelligent and uninterested in his freight, had taken out the newspaper he had bought half an hour previously, and was reading the news pages. He skipped the agony column; which was a pity, because one of its small ads. began: 'Anjli: Am interested in your merchandise. High price if delivered in good condition...' Felder had bought a paper, too; so they knew exactly what the advertisement said. But the dignified and faintly disdainful Sikh didn't look at all like a probable kidnapper.

The passengers from the Madras flight were coming through. A bustling lady in a sari and a woollen coat, with a child in one hand, and transistor in the other, a bandy-legged little husband in a Nehru cap and European suit following with two suitcases; a blasee girl, either English or American, worn-out with sight-seeing and pursued by two porters; a quiet, sensible couple, probably Australian – there must really be something in that legend of easy-going democracy – talking placidly to their one porter as if he lived next door back home, and giving the pleasant impression of effortless enjoyment; and then the flood of southern Indians, small-featured, delicately-built, golden-skinned, alert and aloof, good-humoured people balancing curiosity and self-sufficiency like acrobats. And finally, the Swami Premanathanand, pacing at leisure beside a tall, erect, haughty Punjabi – no mistaking those lofty hawkish lineaments – in the most expensive and yet unobtrusive of tailorings in a neutral tan. They came out through the glass doors

134

talking earnestly, totally absorbed. The stranger was thicker-set than many of the Punjabis Dominic and Tossa had seen, with something of the suavity and goldenness of the Bengali about him, but the jutting nose and flaring nostrils were there, and the fastidious, full-lipped mouth, and the hooded eyes. Bengali eyes have a liquid softness, they suggest reserve but not reticence. These eyes were proud and distant, even, at first encounter, hostile. He had beautifully-cut black hair, crisp and gently wavy, and the sophistication of his movements was what they had expected. The manner of his conversation, urgent, quiet and restrained, tended to bear out everything they had heard or thought of him. He was so well-bred that he might as well have been English.

'That's it!' said Dominic flatly. 'Not much doubt. *He's* genuine!'

The new arrival was brought up standing at sight of the Rolls. It would not have been surprising to see him insert a monocle into his eye to survey it more closely, but he did not. Delicately he stepped up into the back seat, presumably not merely cleared of grain samples for this occasion, but dusted as well; and the Swami mounted beside him as nimbly as ever, twitching the skirt of his robe clear with an expert kick of one heel.

The Rolls turned ponderously, and swept superbly away towards the centre of Delhi.

'All right, driver,' Felder said, at once resigned, puzzled and uneasy. 'Back to Keen's Hotel.' And when they were in motion, not too close to the resplendent veteran sailing ahead: 'Back to square one! It looks like him, and it must be him. Anybody could check the passenger list, after all. So where do we stand now? Don't tell me that driver of his is on the level!'

They didn't tell him anything, one way or the other; it remained an open question all the way back into town.

The Swami brought his friend to Keen's Hotel punctually at half past seven in the evening, apparently deeming it

135

necessary to allow them half an hour for the social niceties before the stroke of eight, when they would all, almost certainly, freeze into strained silence, waiting for the still hypothetical telephone call. Felder, in fact, was the last of the party to arrive, and came in a great hurry from the Connaught Circus office, with a much-handled script under his arm.

'Not that I'm thinking of leaving,' he assured them all, with a tired and rueful smile, 'not until this business of Anjli is cleared up. But I must do a little work sometimes. I hope and pray I'm going to be able to fly back to Benares soon with a clear conscience.' It was easy to see that in spite of his poise the strain was telling on him. He turned to the stranger and held out his hand, not waiting to be formally introduced. 'Mr Kumar, I'm Felder. I expect you know the score about all of us already from the Swami here. I needn't tell you that you have the sympathy of every one of us, and we'll do absolutely everything we can to help you and Anjli out of this mess.'

'I understand from my friend,' said Kumar quietly, 'that you have already done all and more than I could possibly have asked of you. I'm very grateful, believe me. We must set that account straight as soon as possible. But you'll forgive me if my mind can accommodate only one thought at this moment.'

He stood in the middle of Dominic's extravagant hotel sitting-room, immaculate in his plutocratic tailoring, a curiously clear-cut and solitary figure, as if spot-lighted by his deprivation and loneliness on a stage where everyone else was a supernumerary. He was not so tall as they had thought him to be, but his withdrawn and erect bearing accounted for the discrepancy. The patina of wealth was on his complexion, his clothes, his speech, his manner; but that was neither his virtue nor his fault, it was something that had happened to him from birth, and if it had one positive effect, it was to add to his isolation. He was a very handsome man, no doubt of that; the gold of his skin, smoother than silk, devalued whiteness beyond belief. Maybe some

136

day they would get used to that re-estimation of colour, and realise how crude the normal English pink can be.

The Swami, a benevolent stage-manager, set them all an example by seating himself calmly, and composing himself for as long as need be of nerveless waiting. 'We are all of one mind, and all informed about what we have to expect. We have taken all possible steps to deserve success, let us then wait decorously and expect it. We are contemplating an exchange which will be to the advantage and convenience of both parties, there is therefore no need to anticipate double-dealing. It would be worth no one's while.' His practicality sounded, as always, unanswerable; but Kumar, even when he consented to follow his friend's example and sit with folded hands, was tense from crown to heels.

'If the call does come,' ventured Dominic, 'should I answer? And hand it over to you, sir, if it's the same man?'

The Swami approved. 'The number is your number. And there could, of course, be some quite innocent call. Yes, please answer in the first instance.'

It was barely twenty minutes to eight, and the scene was set already. There was nothing now to look forward to but the gradually mounting tension that was going to stretch them all on the same rack until the bell finally rang. Except that they had barely set their teeth to endure the waiting when they were all set jangling like broken puppets, as the innocent white handset emitted its first strident peal of the evening. Never, thought Tossa, huddled in her corner, never, never will I live with a telephone again. Better the telegraph boy at the door every time.

Dominic picked up the receiver. There was sweat trickling down into his eyebrows, prickly as thistles. A voice he hardly knew said distantly: 'Hullo, Dominic Felse here!'

He should have known it was too early, he should have known the damned instrument was going to play with them for the rest of the night. A gentle, courteous, low-pitched voice said in his ear: 'Good, I was afraid you might all be out on the town. I looked in the dining-room, but not a sign of you there. This is Ashok Kabir, I'm down in the foyer.

137

May I come up? I brought a little present for Anjli.'

Distantly Dominic heard himself saying, like an actor reading from a script: 'I wondered why we hadn't heard anything from you. Have you been out of Delhi?'

'Ever since the unit left for Benares. I had three concerts in Trivandrum and Cochin. I'm only just back. Am I inconvenient just now? Maybe you were getting ready to go out. I should have called you from Safdarjung.'

'Anjli...' Dominic swallowed whatever he might have said, looking round all the intent faces that willed him to discretion, and unhappily giving way to their influence. There was only one thing to be done. 'Wait just a moment for me,' he said, 'And I'll come down to you.'

He hung up the telephone, and they could all breathe again. 'It's Ashok,' he said flatly. 'He's just back in town after a concert tour in the south, and it looks as if he doesn't know anything about Anjli being missing. He's brought a present for her, he's expecting to see her. I said I'd go down to him. Now what do I do? Tell him the truth and bring him up here to join us?'

Very placidly, very gently, very smoothly, but with absolute and instant decision, the Swami Premanathanand said: 'No!' It was impossible to imagine him ever speaking in haste, and yet he had got that 'No!' out before anyone else could even draw breath.

'We are five people here already,' he pointed out regretfully, as all eyes turned upon him, 'who know the facts. Five people with whom the vendors have to reckon. I think to let in even one more is to jeopardise our chances of success.'

'I am absolutely sure,' said Tossa, 'that Ashok is to be trusted. He is very fond of Anjli. I know!'

'And I feel sure you are right, but unfortunately that is not the point. He could be the most trustworthy person in the world, and still be enough to frighten off the criminals from dealing with us.'

'He is right,' said Kumar heavily. 'We are already too many, but that cannot be helped. We *can* help adding to the

138

number and increasing the risk.'

Anjli was his daughter, and he was proposing to pay out for her whatever might be needed to bring her back to him safely. There was nothing to be done but respect his wishes.

'Then what do I do? Go down and get rid of Ashok? Tell him Anjli's out? Supposing he's already questioned the clerk on the desk?'

'He would not,' said the Swami absently but with certainty. 'He would question only you, who had the child in charge. Yes, go and talk to him. Tell him Anjli is not here this evening.' He adjusted his glasses, and the great eye from behind the thick lens beamed dauntingly upon the unhappy young face before him. 'Listen,' he said, 'and I will tell you what you shall say to him, if you require from me an act of faith. Put him off for tonight, but invite him to come for coffee tomorrow evening, after dinner ... with you, and Miss Barber here, and Anjli.'

Dominic staring at him steadily for a long moment, considering how deeply he meant it, and realising slowly that the Swami never said anything without deliberate intent. It might not, of course, be the obvious intent, but serious, final and responsible it would certainly be. The only way to find out what lay behind was to go along with him and take the risk.

'All right!' he said. 'That's what I'll tell him.' And he turned and walked out of the room and down the stairs to the foyer where Ashok waited.

It was then just twelve minutes to eight.

Ashok unwrapped the little ivory figure from the piece of grey raw silk in which the carver had swathed it, and set it upright in Dominic's palm. She stood perhaps four inches high, a slender, graceful woman latticed about with lotus shoots and airy curves of drapery, her naked feet in a lotus flower, and a stringed instrument held lovingly in two of her four beautiful arms. Ashok's expressive, long-lashed eyes and deeply-lined gargoyle face brooded over her tenderly.

139

'It is a veena, not a sitar, but Anjli will not mind. This is Saraswati, the mother of the vedas, the goddess of the word, of learning, of all the arts. Perhaps a good person for her to consult, when she finally faces her problem. I found her in a little shop I know in Trivandrum, and I thought Anjli would like her. I am sorry to have missed her, but of course I gave you no notice.'

'I'm sorry about that, too. But if you're free, could you join us here tomorrow night for coffee? About eight o'clock or soon after? We shall all three be very happy to see you then,' he said, setting light to his boats with a flourish; and he did not know whether he was uttering a heartless lie which must find him out in one more day, or committing himself to an act of faith to which he was now bound for life or death. At that moment he did not know whom he trusted or whom he distrusted, he was blind and in the dark, in a landscape totally unfamiliar to him, in which he could find no landmarks. Yet there must, for want of any other beacon, be a certain value in setting a course and holding by it, right or wrong; thus at least you may, by luck rather than judgement, set foot on firm ground at last and find something to hold by.

'Gladly,' said Ashok, 'I shall look forward to it.' He had asked no questions, and even now he asked only one: 'Her father has not yet come to take charge of her?'

'We've heard from him, indirectly,' said Dominic, picking his way among thorns. 'I hope he'll be with her very soon.'

'Good, so it was worth waiting a little.' Ashok nodded his splendid Epstein head in contentment, and picked up his light overcoat, draping it over one shoulder of his grey achkan like a hussar cloak. 'Until tomorrow, then! And my reverences to Miss Barber and Anjli.'

He had a taxi waiting for him in the courtyard, one of the biggest Dominic had ever seen; and at the first step he took into the open air the car came smoothly alongside, placing its rear door-handle confidingly in his hand. That was the kind of service Ashok, for all his reticence and

140

modesty, commanded in Delhi, and probably throughout India, for that matter.

The Swami's Rolls stood in tattered majesty at the end of the ground-floor arcade. The taxi driver gave it a long, respectful look as he turned his own car to drive away, and Ashok, from the rear seat, eyed it even more thoughtfully. Dominic noted, before he turned to go back upstairs in haste, that for once Girish was nowhere in evidence.

The second telephone call came on the stroke of eight, and thereby held up the one for which they were waiting. But the voice that demanded briskly and cheerfully: 'Have you got my co-director there?' was merely that of Ganesh Rao, back from Sarnath a couple of days ahead of schedule with the Deer Park scenes in the can, and anxious to get some early co-operation over the rushes.

'Let me talk to him!' Felder took over the receiver. 'Yes, Felder here! Sure, I'll be out at Hauz Khas in an hour or two, if all goes well. Have you got the whole bunch back safely at the villas? You must have made good time.' In the background he could hear the usual exuberant babel of voices, the girls shrilling and laughing, Channa the charioteer fluting mellifluously, the young American technicians deploying their large, easy drawls, the clinking of glasses, the usual party atmosphere. When he hung up his face was grey with strain; and as soon as the receiver hung in the cradle it pealed again, viciously.

Dominic snatched it from under Felder's hand. This time it must be, this time it had to be, no one could stand much more of this.

'I am calling,' said the unpleasant, clacking old voice, rattling consonants like bones, 'in answer to your advertisement.'

Without a word Dominic held out the receiver to Kumar, who was already stretching out his hand for it. For a moment they could clearly hear the juiceless tones continuing, then Kumar cut them off sharply.

'Listen to me, and let us be clear. I am Kumar. You have

141

what I want, and I am prepared to pay for it. But there will be no deal, there will be no discussion, even, until I have seen for myself that my daughter still lives. Not one rupee until then. No, I will not even speak of money until I am satisfied. You have my word that I have taken no steps to try and trace this call, or to find you, nor shall I do so. If you restore me what I want, neither I nor any of the people here with me will take any action against you. It is my word, it will have to be enough for you. If you cannot trust me far, you must know I cannot trust you at all. You will show my daughter to me, and to these friends of mine who have seen her more recently than I have. You will show her to us in good condition, or you will get nothing. I am a business man, I do not buy pigs in pokes. Then we will talk terms, and arrange an exchange which will protect both of us. You understand me?'

The old voice hectored, rising, growing angry.

'You hold just one saleable article, my friend,' snapped Kumar, 'and I am offering to buy it ... when I have satisfied myself that it is exactly what you are representing it to be. I have promised you we will do no more than that. I have promised you a high price. If you do not want to deal on those terms, where do you think you will find a higher bidder? The circumstances are your problem, not mine. Make up your mind.'

There were brief, acrimonious questions, a note of something like anxiety now in the tone.

'Certainly. If you make it possible, the exchange can take place tomorrow. First let us see her. Then call me here, and I shall make no more difficulties than I must to ensure that she *remains* as we have seen her. There is no question of trust. Each of us must formulate his own safeguards. But do you question that my word is worth more than yours? Make your dispositions, then, we are waiting.'

After that he sat quite silent, listening with admirable concentration and patience for some minutes, the clapper vibrating viciously in his ear. He heaved a long, careful sigh. 'Very well! On behalf of all of us here, I agree.'

142

Very slowly, as if the smoothness and silence of the action mattered vitally, he cradled the receiver, and sat back in his chair with a shivering gasp, wiping his moist hands frenziedly on a vast silk handkerchief.

'Well, it's arranged! Tomorrow, at twelve o'clock, all five of us – oh, yes, whoever he is, he knows how many of us there are! – are to meet for lunch in the first-floor restaurant at Sawyers', on Connaught Circus, near Radial Road Number Five. A window table will be booked for us in advance – in my name! There is a sweet shop just opposite. Promptly at a quarter past twelve Anjli will be brought by taxi to that shop to buy sweets. He says we shall see her clearly. But if any one of us attempts to leave the table and interfere with her, we shall never see her again. And *if* we all obey orders, and finish our lunch and go home, then he will call us again to talk terms and make arrangements for the exchange.'

'And do you believe,' asked Tossa in a whisper, 'that he'll keep his word?'

'I think,' said the Swami Premanathanand, very gently but with complete detachment, 'that he will greatly prefer money and no trouble rather than no money, a dead Anjli and a great deal of trouble. Do you not agree, Mr Felder?'

Felder made a small, protesting sound of revulsion and distaste. Of the impersonal mental processes of India he had had more than enough. 'I think he took her for money, and he'll twist circumstances all the ways he has to, to get money for her. So far he hasn't committed any capital crime, why should he take such a risk now?'

'No capital crime? Well, of course,' said the Swami deprecatingly, 'there is only the little matter of Arjun Baba.'

'Who,' asked Felder simply, 'is Arjun Baba?'

It came as a shock, if a minor shock, to realise that he was in perfectly good faith. They had rushed to confide in him about Anjli, ready to take advantage of sympathy and help wherever it offered, they had mentioned the old man who had been used as a lure for her, but this was the first

143

time Felder had ever actually heard the name of Arjun Baba. Names are powerful magic. That anonymous wisp of India, a puff of grey dust blown away almost unwittingly by the wind of somebody's greed, suddenly put on a man's identity and was illuminated by a man's soul; and suddenly, for the first time, Felder was gazing with horror at the reality of murder.

The Rolls, starting up with somnolent dignity, drove away out of the courtyard with the Swami erect and impassive in the front passenger seat. Kumar, though he had left in company with his friend, was apparently not dependent on him for transport.

'I don't like it!' said Felder, watching the old car round the tall hedge and vanish from view. 'I can't help it, there's something going on that I don't like and don't trust, and there goes the man who's stage-managing the lot of us. It was that driver of his who distracted my attention from the money, just long enough for the parcels to be swopped over. And now tonight, why didn't he want us to let Ashok in on the truth? Why? You saw as well as I did how he jumped in to put his foot on that instantly. Oh, sure it made sense – sense enough for Kumar to echo what he said. And yet – you've seen him at work, he sits there like a god, and nods, and we all do what he says. And now we're all committed to this lunch tomorrow. And *he*'s the one who's pulling the strings!'

'As long as he pulls the one that produces Anjli alive,' said Dominic, shaken but helpless, 'does it matter?'

'No ... if he does that, no, nothing else matters. Not until afterwards, anyhow. No, that's right, we haven't got much choice, have we? She's what matters. Once we've got her back, we can afford to get inquisitive.' His tone said that 'inquisitive' was an under-statement.

'You don't really believe,' whispered Tossa, appalled, 'that the Swami can be behind Anjli's kidnapping? But he's her father's friend. You can see it's true. They've known each other for years.'

144

'That's right! And who knows better than the Swami how much money his friend's good for, and how little he'll miss it? And who can get him to dance to his tune better?'

'But it's crazy! He doesn't care about money. It means nothing to him...' she protested, shaking.

'No, not in dollars, or rupees, or pounds sterling, not one damn' thing. Only in grain seed, and pedigree stock, and agricultural plant, and expert advice... An opportunity's an opportunity, whatever you want the cash for, it doesn't have to be for yourself. *Why didn't he want Ashok to know?* Why was his driver watching me on Sunday, why did he pretend to be an innocent in Delhi, when he knows it like the palm of his hand?'

They laboured to find answers for him, and discovered that they had none for themselves. The thin fingers of the Swami Premanathanand were indeed unobtrusively present in the plot wherever they looked, gently stirring, bringing the mixture to the boil.

'Our hands are tied, anyhow,' said Dominic flatly. 'If he really is behind the whole affair, then he genuinely intends to hand over Anjli tomorrow. And there's nothing we can do except go along with him until she's safe.'

On which exceedingly chilly comfort they separated for the night, Felder to the villa at Hauz Khas where Ganesh Rao was waiting with the rushes from Sarnath, and Tossa and Dominic to a belated sandwich and a lime soda in the bar, and then a solitary walk round the quiet streets near the Lodi Park. It was the walk that completed their sense of disorientation and confusion; for they returned by way of Aurangzeb Road, and passing by the drive of Claridge's, were just in time to see one of the handsome, well-groomed, well-heeled couples of Delhi strolling arm-in-arm from the hotel to the taxi rank. A good-looking, austere, proud, pale Punjabi in a European suit, and a very lovely woman in a white and gold sari on his arm, her towering beehive of lustrous black hair defying fashion, which one so beautiful could well afford to ignore. There was nothing indecorous about them, they were talking together gravely and quietly,

145

their faces intent. There was nothing about them, indeed, to excite any feelings but those of pleasure and admiration – except that the man was Satyavan Kumar, and the woman – once seen, never forgotten – was Kamala, whom they knew best as Yashodhara, the bride of Prince Siddhartha, the Buddha.

X

Anjli sat on a string bed in a tiny room about eight feet
square, lit by one little smoky window far above her head.
It was the fourth day she had spent in this place, and she
knew every article in the room, every fine crinkle of cracks
in the dun-coloured plaster of the walls, every crease in the
garish almanack pinned above the rickety wooden chest.
The ceiling was disproportionately high, the floor of rough
concrete with one threadbare cotton rug. On the bed was a
thin flock mattress, and a grey blanket. The chest of
drawers was of thickly varnished and heavily scratched
wood, dark red, with an artificial silk cover in several
violent colours spread over it, and above it the smooth,
effeminate blue Krishna smiling over his flute with those
kind, mischievous, amoral, dangerous eyes of his, the eyes
of a fairy rather than a god. Propped on the gay cover were
one faded family photograph, so faint now that it had nothing to say to her, not even whether the persons in it were
male or female, and one picture of Sri Ramakrishna, cut
from a newspaper and stuck askew in a carved wooden
frame.

There was nothing else in the room. And all three of
them slept there at night, the two little girls on the string
bed, the woman on a rug spread on the floor beside them.

This was not the whole of Anjli's present world, however. She could pass at will through the single door of the
room, or most of the time she could do so; but that would
merely bring her into a short clay-coloured passage, locked
against her at the nearer end, and at the other leading only
to two even tinier rooms, the first an Indian bathroom, a
concrete box just big enough to stand up in, with a cold
water tap on the wall and a drain in the centre of the gently
sloping floor, the second a flush lavatory, eastern style, with

a porcelain basin sunk in the floor and two raised platforms for the feet. There the passage ended in another locked door. But she thought that wherever she might be, she was on the ground floor, for at the minute window of the lavatory leaves leaned down to her at an angle which suggested the lowest branches of a tree.

This was all she knew, and after four days she knew it like the palm of her hand; but she could not deduce from it anything that might be useful to her.

There was nothing the matter with Anjli's mind or memory, she was not too much afraid to sift detail from detail and build them laboriously into a picture of her days, but the picture could never be complete, for this place of her confinement was a bubble, without a material location at all. She remembered perfectly the gleam of the old man's eyes across the brazier, the instant flash of intelligence that warned her this was not Arjun Baba, and spurred her into flight. She remembered the sickening half-suffocation under the folds of the blanket, the struggles that wasted themselves feebly, and soon ceased when she realised that she was in a van in motion. She had not lost consciousness at all, but face-down in her odorous wrappings on the floor of the van, with no light, and the vehicle turning and circling and dodging to complete her confusion, she had lost all sense not only of direction but of distance. Towards the end she had lapsed into something close to a faint, starved for air. Now she did not know even whether she was still in Delhi, much less in which part of it.

Two people between them had carried her in from the van, she thought by the locked door beyond the lavatory, but even of that she could not be sure. All she could be certain of was that they had released her from her wrappings in this room, the old man and the woman between them, and here she had been ever since, watched and guarded.

The old man she saw seldom, he came only now and again to make sure that his catch was still safe. During his few visits she had studied him closely, because she had now

148

no resources but her own ingenuity, and the only food she had for that was observation. The more she recorded, the more chance that some day she might find a weak place in the fortress and its garrison. But she felt from the beginning that it would not be in the old man. Now that she came to study him at close quarters she saw that he was not at all like Arjun Baba, and certainly not nearly so old and frail. This one, grizzled and bent though he might be, and tangled in a wealth of beard, would have made two of Satyavan's pensioner. He was broad-shouldered, sturdy and muscular, and she had already experienced the strength of his arms and hands. He had a harsh, querulous, irascible old voice that grated unpleasantly on the air and even more unpleasantly on the mind, suggesting as it did a short temper, and a nature subject to malice and panic. He spoke to her not at all, not even one word. It was to the woman he talked, hectoring, bullying and demanding, in Hindi. And the woman did everything he ordered, in cringing haste and for the best of reasons, because she was afraid of him.

It seemed to be the woman who lived here. She was much younger than the man. She looked, perhaps, fifty, but there were factors which caused Anjli to reason that in reality she must be considerably younger still; notably there was the girl, who seemed to be about Anjli's own age, give or take a year, and yet was almost certainly this woman's daughter. So it wasn't time, it was circumstances that had aged the mother. She was painfully thin and worn, her features blurred by timidity and hopelessness, the only rich thing about her her great coil of dark brown hair. She wore blouses and saris of plain cotton dyed in single colours, and so faded with washing that the once brilliant red had ebbed to a streaked and withered rose. When the old man was there she was a quivering, wary creature obsequious to his every gesture and word, and yet in some insinuating way she seemed to place herself between his possible animosity and Anjli. And when he was not there she was timid and gentle, she offered food with consideration, she left the bed to the children; but she was too cowed ever to be an ally, and too much afraid of the old man ever to forget to lock a door.

Her cooking was done somewhere outside. Anjli pictured a lean-to shed in a corner of a small compound, with pots hissing gently over the inevitable charcoal braziers, such as she had seen in the modest residential areas of Rabindar Nagar. Altogether, there was something about this woman's living quarters which did not suggest the most primitive poverty, by any means, poor though she undoubtedly was. A certain respectability and security existed here. Some-body's housekeeper, perhaps? The old man's? But no, he did not live here, she was almost certain of that. And what sort of place was it, in any case? These rooms were so enclosed that traffic noises did not penetrate. She could not even guess at the kind of road or street that lay outside her prison.

And then there was the girl. Late in the afternoon of the first day she had manifested herself, first as a young, curious voice plying the woman with questions, some-where beyond the locked door. And surely there had been a low, continuous hum as background to their exchanges, a sound which made itself known in retrospect as the purr of a vacuum cleaner? Anjli could never be quite sure about that, but perhaps only because the idea seemed to her so fantastic. She forgot about it, in any case, when the woman unlocked the door and the girl came sliding through it, and stood staring, mute with shyness, at her mysterious con-temporary.

Her name was Shantila, for Anjli had heard her mother call her so. She was learning English at school; but as yet she spoke it very haltingly, and indeed for the most part, even in her own language, was a very taciturn child. Life had not encouraged her to be voluble. She was a couple of inches shorter than Anjli, but otherwise they were well-matched in size, as was soon demonstrated; for on his next visit the old man had issued his orders, and Anjli had forthwith been given some of Shantila's school clothes to wear instead of her own jersey suit. White shalwar and

150

deep blue kameez, and the inevitable gauze scarf in white. Would a country school make use of such a uniform, or could she rely on it that she was still in Delhi? No use asking Shantila, she had all too clearly been told to avoid such subjects. Probably she had even been told to keep away from the prisoner. She vanished whenever the old man was there. But in his absence the attraction was too great. Shantila was free to pass through the locked doors if she wished; but after a day Anjli began to understand how barren a freedom this was to her. The most fascinating and wonderful thing in her world drew her inward into Anjli's captivity.

At first she simply sat and stared, devouring with her eyes every facet of the strange girl's strangeness, the supple leather shoes in their antique leather shades melting from deep red to mouse-brown, the delicate silvery-pink colouring of the woollen jacket and skirt, the finger-nails shaped and tinted like rose petals, all the exotic accoutrements of Anjli's westernness. On the second day, approaching with daring shyness, she began to touch, to stroke the kitten-softness of the angora and lambswool jersey, and even the smooth texture of Anjli's lacquered nails.

They arrived at a kind of understanding almost without words. Shantila shook her head nervously when she was questioned, so why question her? What she let fall unwittingly might be worth much more. Moreover, Anjli found that she could not pursue a creature so wary, and with such evident reasons for her fears. This was not and never could be an enemy, and there are measures which are inadmissible except with enemies. Even her own desperate need to act in her own defence did not alter that.

She knew, of course, what must be the reason for her abduction. There could be only one. She was the child of money, and someone intended to get money in exchange for her. The trouble was that she was too sophisticated to conclude that that in any way guaranteed her safety; she knew of too many cases to the contrary. But so far, at least, she was hoarded like treasure, and with luck she might yet have time to find a means to help herself. But preferably not at Shantila's expense.

They slept together on the sagging bed at night, and drew delicately apart when they inadvertently touched, with a kind of mutual respect that could have arisen in no other circumstances; and then, when they touched of intent, in search of a mysterious measure of comfort, they did not withdraw.

And this was the fourth morning. The sun was already high, for the leaves that whirled and span just within view from the lavatory window were gilded through. Shantila had come home from school, and had no more classes that day. They ate their mid-day food together, and Shantila sat content as on the first day to watch and wonder. For her Anjli was inexhaustible. Even now that the fabulous clothes were gone, the glamour had not departed. And there was still her necklace and polished round beads, in a dozen melting shades of brown and grey and green. Shantila had no jewellery; even her mother had only two or three thin glass bangles to her name.

Anjli saw how the huge, hungry brown eyes dwelt on her necklace, not coveting, only marvelling, satisfied with contemplation because there was no further possibility. Dorette had brought the beads back for her once from Scotland, they were only the subtle semi-precious pebbles of the Scottish hills, rounded and polished and strung into a neat little choker, eminently suitable for a young girl. What they were to Shantila she saw suddenly in a wonderful, inverted vision, the jewels from the ends of the earth. They had no value until you realised they had a transferable value, and then they were beyond price. How stupid, then, that they should stay where they were worthless, when they could so easily go where they were treasure.

Anjli put up her hands to the back of her neck, and undid the silver clasp.

'Turn round, let me put it on for you.'

She lowered the chain of stones to Shantila's neck, and Shantila drew back from it instinctively, shaking her head

152

in fright and putting up a hand to fend off the gift.

'No ... no ... they are yours ...'

'No, they are for you. I want to give them to you. If you like them? You *do* like them?' She said simply: 'I have others.' And she thought: 'I *had* others!' and wondered when, if ever, she would see them again.

Shantila's eyes, still dubious but unable to lie, shone huge as moons with pleasure. Anjli fastened the clasp, and stood back to look at the effect, and Shantila's awed fingertips explored the cold round smoothness of bead after bead in astonishment and delight. The two girls looked at each other long and steadily, in recognition and wonder and satisfaction over the exchange of something undefined, the completion of some bargain in which both of them had gained.

They were so engrossed in their own mutual discoveries that they had not remarked the voices raised outside in the passage. The sudden opening of the door, the apparition of the old man on the threshold, massive head sunk into the brown shawl he wore round his shoulders, shook them apart with a disagreeable shock, as though they had only now realised his possible significance to them both.

'Come, Anjli,' said the ancient, gravelly voice, with a horrid note of ingratiation that matched the fond, false smile on the bearded face. 'You are going shopping with us.'

He took her by one wrist before she could even reason whether there was any sense in resisting, or indeed anything to be feared in complying. The woman, shrinking at his shoulder, obediently took her other arm. Shantila ventured to follow them uneasily along the passage to the rear door, but then the old man turned his head and scowled her back, and she stood motionless where they had left her, watching them go.

It was the first time Anjli had ever seen this narrow wooden door opened. It brought them out into dazzling sunshine in a small, high-walled yard, the sparkling leaves

of one tree leaning over the wall. There were two or three
sheds, as she had expected; there was a car of unobtrusive
age and make standing in the shade; and just outside the
open yard gates, in a narrow lane, there was an unmistakable Delhi taxi waiting for them.

They put her into the middle of the back seat between
them, the woman holding her left arm, the man her right;
and as the taxi began to move, the man twitched her scarf
dexterously round her eyes, and blinded her until they were
well away from the house and the yard. She did not resist;
and in a moment he let her emerge, for though there was no
disguising Delhi, one Delhi street is like enough to another
to confuse all those who do not know it well.

So they were still in the city, that was something gained.
Anjli sat silent but tense between them, watching and thinking. What was to happen now? Had she already been ran-
somed, and was she now to be set at liberty? She could not
trust too easily in any such optimistic assessment of her
position. Then why? Had her hiding-place become unsafe,
and was she to be transferred to another? Then she had
better be ready to seize even the least chance that might
offer, here in the streets. Anything could be true, except, of
course, that they were simply going shopping.

They drove for some while in the spacious streets of the
new town, but never could she find a firm landmark; and
when at length the driver brought them to the sweet shop
opposite Sawyers' Restaurant, he did so by the nearest of
the radial roads, so that the long, smooth, crescent curve of
Connaught Circus should not be obvious.

The car drew up closely to the curb.

'Come,' beamed the old man, 'we are going here. To buy
some sweets for you and for Shantila. You will be very
quiet and sensible, will you not, Anjli? For your father's
sake, remember that!'

She could have outrun them both, but they never let go
of her wrists. And there was no one close, to whom she
could call, no traffic policeman, no passing English tourist.
She stood for a moment hanging back between them on the

154

broad pavement, and looked all round her with one rapid glance at the shining day that offered her no help; a Delhi schoolgirl of fourteen in shalwar and kameez, out shopping with her mother and grandfather. Who was going to give her a second look? She yielded to the pull of their hands, and went with them into the shop.

'Yes,' said Dominic, leaning over Tossa's chair to strain his eyes after the slight figure vanishing under the shop awning, 'that's Anjli!'

'You are quite sure? It's so long,' said Kumar defensively, 'since I saw her.'

'Quite sure,' said Tossa.

'It's Anjli, all right,' Felder confirmed, and his voice shook with tension. 'Now, for God's sake, what do we do?'

'Exactly what we promised,' said the Swami Premanathanand gently, not even leaning forward in his chair. 'We remain here, making no move to alarm her captors. We wait for further word. So far, you will agree, they have kept their part of the bargain.'

'But, damn it, she's there, right under our eyes, and only those two decrepit people to keep her from us . . . if we went straight down now, and into the shop after them . . .' Felder mopped sweat from his seamed forehead, and breathed heavily.

'We were also warned that if we made any such move we might never see her again,' the Swami pointed out gently, and sipped his soup. 'We cannot take such a risk. We must abide by our side of the bargain, too. For her sake.'

'I suppose you're right.' Felder subsided with a vast and bitterly reluctant sigh.

'They're coming out,' whispered Tossa.

All three linked, as before, both Anjli's arms prisoned. The box of sweets they had bought was carried under the old man's arm. Helplessly the five in the first-floor window of Sawyers' watched the trio move unhurriedly to the edge of the pavement, and saw the Sikh taxi-driver lean to open

155

the rear door for them. First the woman vanished within, then the child, then the old man. The door closed on them with a brisk bang.

'We *can't* . . .' breathed Felder. But none of them moved. The Swami sat erect, a small, rueful smile curving his lips. The noon traffic round Connaught Circus swirled placidly, thinning for the siesta. Into the scattered stream the taxi moved gracefully, like a floating leaf, caught the full current and was away. A garishly-decorated scooter-taxi brushed by it in the opposite direction, and another as gay let it pass at a side-street before turning off. A few cars swung here and there in the dance. Out of a garage yard a more powerful motorbike-taxi sailed with a roar, dark green awning flapping, and rocketed away in the same direction Anjli and her escort had taken.

The Swami appeared to be watching nothing, and to see nothing, but he had in his mind a complete map of all these complex traffic movements. Everyone else was staring frantically, but none of them observed the one significant thing which had happened. For the driver of the motorbike rickshaw, had he not been as invisible to them as all the other casual service personnel of Delhi, the postmen, the peons, the porters, would have been recognised at once as Girish, his master's monumental Rolls for once abandoned. Girish had made no promises, and taken part in no bargain. Girish was a free agent.

The taxi proceeded without haste round the curve of Connaught Circus, the motorcycle-rickshaw followed at a nicely-judged distance. There could hardly be a better instrument for pursuit in Delhi, where in any street of the new town at any time of the day you may see at least three or four of them, all looking much alike. Nobody pays any attention to them, unless he wishes to hire one, and even then it is not unusual to watch them sail disdainfully by, for in the deep shade of their awnings it is difficult to be sure whether they are occupied or not. Nor does anyone turn a hair at seeing them driven at crazy speeds, so that even an alerted quarry might have great trouble in getting away from them. Girish, however, had no intention of betraying himself. His object was to trail them to their destination, not to overhaul them. He hung back by fifteen yards or so, driving obliquely behind the taxi so that he should not become obtrusive in the driving mirror, allowing other vehicles to intervene now and then, varying the pattern of his pursuit, the big machine idling happily under him. He foresaw no trouble. All he needed to know was where they were holding her, and then the rest was up to him. In the meantime he did not mean to make any mistake.

Nor was what happened next due to any error on his part. It was something against which he could not possibly have taken precautions.

In the back of the taxi Anjli sat between her guards, quivering with tension and aware that time was running out. They were on their way back to the tiny, obscure dwelling in the quiet yard, and once they reached it she would have lost her only opportunity. This inexplicable trip back into the world, on the face of it completely senseless, must mean something, if only she could grasp what. Had she merely been removed from the place for a brief while because someone dangerous was expected there? Had she been put back into apparent circulation simply to show her to someone, to disarm suspicions of who or what she was? It had to mean something that could help her to know how to act, and here were the minutes and seconds dwindling through her fingers, and nothing gained. Uneasily she craned on all sides, searching the pavements that unrolled beside her. The old man had loosed his hold on her. She turned and swept her hand across the dusty rear window, peering back along their track. She saw the motorcycle-rickshaw that should have meant nothing to her, the long, slim, lightly-balanced body of its driver; she saw, and studied for one broken moment with astonished passion, the lean, aquiline face with its bold bones and intent, proud eyes fixed unmistakably on the car that carried her.

She uttered a shriek of exultation, and whirled to pound

157

with both fists upon the Sikh driver's shoulder. 'Stop!' she cried, in a voice of such authority that his foot instinctively went down on the brake. 'Stop, at once!'

The old man had her by the arm again by then, though it took him all his time to hold her. She had not lost her instinct for the last chance; when the driver braked they were all three flung forward in the seat, and she reached across the frightened woman and tore at the handle of the door, willing to push the woman out before her and jump for it if only they gave her time.

She was just too late. 'Drive on, drive on, quickly!' bellowed the man beside her, and all the cracked tones of age had fallen away from his voice in this crisis. 'Don't listen to me. You see she is ill ... she is mad ... we must get her home...' The car lurched forward again powerfully and gathered speed, and Anjli was flung back helplessly into the cushions. The woman was sobbing with excitement and dread. The man cursed her savagely, cursed Anjli with even more heartfelt passion, and crouched scowling through the back window. He knew now that they were followed. She had done the one thing she should not have done.

'Faster, faster! There is a motorcycle-rickshaw following us. You must lose him ... you must! I promise you double your fare if you get us back safely.'

They were threading traffic at speed now, taking flagrant risks to put other vehicles between them, whirling dangerously out of the main stream, plunging through side-streets, Anjli was lost again, the city went round her like a kaleidoscope. She tried to pull herself up to the window, and the old man took her by her braid of hair and thrust her down again. She struck at him with all her strength, clenched her fingers in his beard and tugged. Spitting curses, he took her by the wrists and unlaced her fingers by force, one by one.

'Faster, faster ... this bullock-cart... Quickly, pass it, and it will block the way for him! Yes, *now*! No, no, not to the back, drop us at the front here, there is no time...'

The taxi hurtled to a halt, groaning, the doors were flung open, and Anjli dragged out, dishevelled and panting, and

158

hustled across a narrow garden and in at a fan-lighted door. She heard money change hands hurriedly, enough money to close the taxi-driver's mouth. She heard the car accelerate in haste and dash away. The outer door slammed again upon the old man. He came into the cool, bare white office in which she stood with the shivering woman, a bristling caricature of fury and terror, dripping words like acid, holding his head as if it ached beyond bearing.

So now, too late, she knew. She knew where she was, where she had been all these four days. That tall, Victorian-colonial facade she was not likely to forget, nor the little garden and the low hedge before it. If they had not been forced for lack of time to come in by the front way she might never have recognised the place. Outside that door she had waited with her friends for Ashok Kabir, on the first evening in Delhi. All this time she had been held prisoner in the caretaker's quarters of the film company's Delhi office and store, on Connaught Circus.

And now that she had begun to make discoveries, it seemed there was no end to the things she knew. She knew that the old, cracked voice, when shaken out of its careful impersonation by a crisis, grew full and resonant and loud. She knew that when she had clenched her fingers in his beard what he had felt had not been pain, but only alarm; why else should he have disengaged her hold so carefully, instead of hitting out at her with all his force?

She let him come close to her, the awful, bitter, incomprehensible words nothing to her now. She stood like a broken-spirited child until he was within her reach, and then she lunged with both hands, not at his beard this time, but at the thick bush of grey hair, bearing down with all her weight, ripping it from his head. Wig and beard came away together in her clutch, tearing red, grazed lines across his cheeks and brows where they had been secured. Nothing remained of the senile elder but two round, grained grey patches of make-up on his cheeks, the carefully-painted furrows on his forehead, and the tangle of hair that Anjli let fall at his feet, curled on the floor like a

159

sleeping Yorkshire terrier. What was left was a sturdy man in his thirties, high-complexioned, smooth-featured, with close-cropped black hair.

'Now I know you,' she said, without triumph, for she knew that she had made an enemy in a sense in which she had never had an enemy before. 'You are not just an old man, you are *Old Age. Old Age and Death.* I even remember your name. Your name is Govind Das.' And suddenly and peremptorily she demanded, as if it emerged now as the most important thing in the world, and the most crucial issue between them: '*What have you done with Arjun Baba?*'

XI

Govind Das took two lurching steps towards her, and beneath his red-brown skin the blood ebbed, leaving him dull
and grey as clay. The woman, shivering and pleading, edged
a timid shoulder between the two, and he took her by her
sari with a clumsy, violent gesture, and flung her out of his
way. He gripped Anjli's arm, and dragged her away out of
the empty office, back to the locked door beside the little
living-room, the woman following all the way, her eyes
great with terror, her tongue stumbling through agonised
protests. It seemed she might even raise the courage to defy
him, but Anjli knew she never would, she had been under
his thumb too long.

The key was in the living-room door, he turned it and
pushed Anjli blindly within, so awkwardly that she fell
against the edge of the bed. For one moment she had caught
a glimpse of the lavatory door being drawn gently but
rapidly to, as Shantila hid herself within. Shantila knew
about anger, and had learned to withdraw herself out of its
reach; and this by its very quietness was no ordinary storm.

The key turned in the lock again. She had gained nothing, she was back in the old prison. Another key grated;
the door at the end of the passage, the door through which
she had just been dragged from the offices, was secured
against her. And somewhere beyond it broke out the most
horrifying dialogue of rage and pleading and despair she
had ever heard. She understood not one word, and yet she
understood everything that mattered; she knew that this
was crucial, and that her own fate now depended on the
outcome. The man raved and threatened, and even more
shatteringly burst into desperate tears; the woman urged,
coaxed, wept, argued, even protested. Sometimes, Anjli
thought, listening with her cheek against the door, Govind

Das struck her, but still she did not give up.

Crouching thus to the keyhole, she heard a soft step in the corridor, and the steadying touch of a light hand against the wall. Shantila, too, was listening there, and Shantila understood what they were saying. Anjli drew a deep, steadying breath, and waited. She dared not speak. Probably these two would hear nothing until they had fought out to the end this tremendous battle over her, but she dared not take the risk.

Very softly and cautiously the key began to turn in the lock, and inch by inch the door swung open. In the doorway Shantila beckoned, the fingers of one hand pressed to her lips.

'Quickly!' It was only the hurried ghost of a whisper, urging her. 'You must go ... my uncle is afraid now ... you've seen him now, you know him, you can tell about him ...'

Anjli crept to her side. They stood for an instant almost cheek to cheek, listening.

'He wants to kill you,' Shantila's lips shaped soundlessly, 'so that you cannot tell. They told him, keep you safe, not hurt you ... but now he's afraid ...'

The careful disguise of Old Age, and all his expertise in the part, had been no protection to him in the end.

They edged their way silently into the corridor, and carefully Shantila re-locked the door. With held breath they tiptoed past the bathroom and the lavatory, and gingerly turned the last key that let them out into the sunshine of the compound.

The heavy wooden doors were locked, but the thick crossbars and the iron stanchion that held them in place made good aids for climbing, and they were both lightweights and agile. Anjli hauled herself up to the top of the gate and straddled it, leaning down to offer a hand to Shantila scrambling after her. Through the leaves of the single tree the noonday sunlight sprinkled the film company's old utility with gold. And somewhere within the rear premises of the old house a man's voice uttered a great, mangled howl of terror and dismay.

'Quick, give me your hand!' Anjli hauled strongly, and in a moment they lay gasping together over the crest of the gate. The rickety wooden door they had locked behind them shook and groaned to the impact of a heavy body, reverberated again and again, but held fast. The two girls scrambled over the gate and lowered themselves to hang by their hands. Shantila fell neatly on her feet, Anjli grazed her elbow against the rough wood and left a smear of blood on her sleeve. Behind them a window on the first floor opened, a deep sash-window that gave on the flat roof of the bathroom, and Govind Das came leaping through it with a convulsed face, and eyes half-mad with fear and hate, and let himself down in a scrambling fall to the compound. He saw, and they knew he had seen, the small, clenched fingers loose their hold on the crest of the gate. He heard, and they knew he heard, their light feet running like hares away down the crooked lane, and out into the street.

It was not for comfort they took hands and matched their steps; it was so that neither of them should be the fleeter, for now they were one creature in one danger, and there could not possibly be any half salvation.

The iron strut of the compound gates rattled against the wall, the unlocked gates hurtled wide and shuddered to the impact. In a moment the engine of the film company's utility started into life, and Govind Das drove it out into the lane, and away at high speed towards Connaught Circus, where Anjli and Shantila fled from him hand in hand.

Round the corner in Parliament Street, where the spacious side-walks and the green shade trees began, traffic was indulging in its midday siesta, only an occasional car rolling at leisure down the wide, straight road. Screened by a little grove of bushes, a telephone kiosk sat in the green border between road and pathway. A large motorcycle-rick-shaw with a deep green awning was parked beside it, and within the box Girish had just dialled the number of

Sawyers' restaurant, and was talking to the Swami Premanathanand.

'I lost them. Bad luck with a bullock wagon. But I overtook the same taxi only a minute later, going on round the Circus from here towards Irwin Road, empty. They're somewhere in this block, right on the Circus, between Janpath and Parliament Street. Yes, I'm certain. I know his number. I'll get the police to pick up the driver, and when he finds out what he's up against he'll surely talk, for his own sake.'

He was listening to the Swami's brisk reply, and gazing out through the glass panels of his kiosk when everything happened at once. Past him down Parliament Street from the Circus came two young girls in identical white shalwar and blue kameez, gauze scarves flying. They held hands, and ran like athletes, with set faces and floating plaits, ran as if for their lives. Unwisely but understandably, they had chosen to run in the roadway, because there was almost no traffic, and the few saunterers on the paths would have held them up to some extent. But even one car is enough to be dangerous, especially one driven as crazily as this black veteran coming hurtling down behind them from the circus. You'd have thought he was actually trying to run the children down . . .

Girish made never a sound. The telephone receiver dropped from his hand and swung for a moment, distilling the Swami's dulcet tones into empty air. The door of the kiosk hurtled open and slammed shut with a force that broke one pane of glass, and before the pieces had finished tinkling to the floor, Girish was astride his motorcycle and had kicked it into life and motion. He sailed diagonally across Parliament Street, straight into the path of the oncoming car. The girls were hardly ten yards ahead when the impact came, and they leaped tormentedly forward like hares pursued, and never looked behind.

Govind Das saw from the corner of his eye the heavy rickshaw surge forward, bent on ramming him. He had just enough sanity and just enough driving instinct left to take the only avoiding action possible. He swung the wheel to the left, to minimise the crash, and the motor cycle took him obliquely in the right front wing and swept the car onward into the grass belt between roadway and path. In an inextricable mass of metal the two vehicles lurched to a stop, and subsided in a dissolution of plates and parts, the horrid noise eddying away in diminishing echoes between the trees. In the stunned moments before anyone came running, Govind Das dragged himself dizzy but uninjured out of the driving seat, and slid away hastily from the scene. A car stolen from the film company's premises ... a reckless driver ... a crash ... what was there new in that? All he had to do was take care of the girl, and then get back and report the car missing.

He could still see the two little figures in blue and white, well ahead now. They had made a mistake, they were heading for the great iron gates of the Jantar Mantar Park, down there on the left of the road. He needn't even hurry.

He looked back once, and the driver of the motorcycle – was he crazy, or something? Govind Das didn't even know him, had never set eyes on him before! – still lay in the road, huddled beside the wreckage. Dead or alive, did it matter? No doubt an ambulance would be along for him in a matter of minutes, as soon as someone grasped what had happened here. Govind Das turned contentedly, and loped gently after Anjli Kumar, towards the park gates from which there was no escape. This wall would be too high for them to climb.

Girish had swung his legs clear of the machine and jumped just before the moment of impact, but the impetus of his rush had carried him into the wing of the car just the same, though with less violence. He hit the road hard and flatly, knocking the breath out of his body, and his head struck the metal of the car body with enough force to stun him for some seconds. He opened his eyes upon the gravelly surface of the road, one cheek skinned, the grains of dust like boulders against his lips; but the first painful move-

165

ments assured him he was alive, and had no breakages.
Dazedly he drew up his knees under him, and raised himself from the road.

There had been no one very close to the scene of the
crash, but from both directions now people were coming on
the run. Hastily Girish withdrew himself behind the crumpled bulk of the two vehicles, and melted backwards into
the shelter of the trees. Easy to vanish here, and he had no
time to answer police questions, not yet, not until those
children were recovered alive. They had disappeared
utterly from view now. He removed himself far enough
from the wreck to escape notice, and then moved out into
the roadway and stared ahead down the long, straight vista
of Parliament Street. They were nowhere in sight, yet he
could not believe that they had run so far ahead in the time.
There were two possible turns off, somewhat ahead but still
possible, Jai Singh Road on the right, and the lane opposite
to it. And before that, of course, there was the gate into the
park.

That made him look to the left, where the iron filigree of
the gates stood open in their high wall. He was just in time
to see Govind Das turn in towards the gravelled paths of
the gardens, limping slightly, in no haste. Until ten minutes
ago he had never seen that man in his life, but he could not
see him now, even at this distance, without knowing him
again.

Girish wiped the smears of blood from his face with a
crumpled handkerchief, and set off at an unsteady trot after
his quarry.

The Jantar Mantar is the oddest monument of Delhi,
and one of the most charming, though without guide-book
or guide you might wander round it for days and be no
nearer guessing at its purpose. It looks as if some highly
original modern sculptor-architect, in love with the space-
age, had set to work to decorate this garden with the shapes
of things to come. In reality the buildings are nearly two
hundred and fifty years old, but it is no illusion that their

166

creator was in love with space. For this is just one of the five giant observatories built around India by the Maharajah Jai Singh the Second, of Jaipur, town-planner and astronomer extraordinary, in the early eighteenth century. Six immense masonry instruments, nobly spaced through the fine gardens with which the Indians inevitably surround every antiquity, tower even above the royal palms. Their shapes are as beautiful as they are functional – or as they were functional in their heyday – and their colour is a deep, soft rose, picked out here and there with white, so that their cleanness and radiance adds to the fantasy of their forms. A pair of great, roofless, rose-coloured towers, each with a stone column in the centre, each with its walls regularly perforated by empty window-niches, once recorded the ascension and declension of the stars. A structure like half a giant rosy fruit lies obliquely tilted, white seeds of staircases glistening within its rind. Two lidless concrete ink-wells open their dark interiors to the sun, and several short staircases invite visitors to mount and walk round their rims. There are stairs everywhere, even some shut within enclosing walls and apparently inaccessible from any point. There are doors hanging halfway up sheer old-rose walls, with no visible way to them. There are open rectangles of snowy concrete like dancing-floors, and curved projections of stone like hands cupping and measuring shadow. And all around these giants lie watered lawns punctuated with flowering shrubs, long herbaceous borders flanking the red gravel paths, and tall royal palms, their smooth trunks swathed in silver-grey silk.

Into this superb fantasy the two girls darted, still blown on the winds of terror and resolution, but running out of breath. A few people strolled ponderously along the gravel paths, a few clambered about the many staircases, one or two sat on retired benches in the shade, placidly eating sandwiches. But they seemed so few, and so unreal, as though someone had put them in, carefully arranged, to complete the dream. It seemed impossible that one could approach and speak to them, and actually be heard and

167

answered. Anjli's stunned senses recorded but could not believe in the wonders she saw. She knew nothing about primitive instruments of astronomy, and had had no notion of what awaited her within the wall. She had a stitch in her side, and her chest was labouring, she had to stop. Here among the trees, and under these gigantic shadows, surely they could elude one man, even if he followed them here. And if he passed by, all they had to do was wait, and venture out when it seemed safe, and take a scooter-taxi to Keen's Hotel. She had no money, her bag had been taken from her along with her own clothes, but the driver would not ask for payment until he brought them to their destination.

'I've got to rest,' she said, gulping air, 'I can't run any more.'

'Come farther,' urged Shantila, quaking, 'come to the trees. There he won't see us.'

They took the left-hand path, which stretched straight ahead from the gate, because it led to groves where they could lurk in cover and still watch the gateway. They walked now, though in haste and with many glances behind, stumbling a little from pure weariness of spirit rather than of body. They passed the rosy, petrified fruit the giant's child had dropped, a pomegranate full of white steps for seeds. The most awe-inspiring of all Jai Singh's immense conceptions hung over them. They saw it from this angle as a lofty needle of stone, sailing sheer out of the ground for nearly sixty feet, with a round drum of stone on the top. It looked like a monolith, but as they hurried forward they drew alongside it, and saw that this sheer face was actually the shortest side of a right-angled triangle laid on its edge. Upwards by the hypotenuse, breathtakingly steep, a lady in a sari was proceding towards the summit, plodding stolidly, a flutter of blue and white silk. One more staircase for all game tourists to climb, the most daunting of them all. The containing walls that protected her scarcely reached her knees. At the top there was no handrail at all round the sheer drop of nearly sixty feet, and perhaps two feet of clearance all round the stone drum.

Anjli stumbled towards the bushes and sanctuary, suddenly terribly tired, oppressed even more by these unforeseen and incomprehensible marvels than by her own half-digested experiences. She had not the least idea that she was staring at the monumental gnomon of one of the biggest sundials in the world, Jai Singh's 'Prince of Dials'. If someone had tried to explain it to her then, she would not have understood. She was very close to the limit of her forces, and only too deeply aware that Shantila, loyal and loving as she might be, could not help her any more. They had reverted to their basic simplicity. It was a long time since Anjli had felt herself a child.

In the green coolness and dimness under the trees, themselves hidden, they found a seat where they could watch the gate. A few people came and went, but several of them were gardeners. Always, in Indian gardens, there are almost more gardeners than visitors. Anjli sat forward and cradled her head in her arms until her breath came more easily; and a terrible drowsiness laid hold of her and smoothed her eyelids closed.

Shantila's sharp little elbow stabbed her side. She heard the first indrawn breath of panic. 'He has come! He knows we are here!'

Anjli jerked up her head and rose to peer tensely through the leaves. There was no mistake. The incongruous head, short black hair still ruffled from under the wig of Old Age, cheeks marked by round grey patches of make-up and forehead seamed with false wrinkles, leaned forward like a hound on a scent, probing down this very path which they had chosen as a way to safety.

They clung together, hesitating far too long. If they had run at once, clean across between the instruments to the other side of the garden, they could have got back to the gate unobserved. Even if they had withdrawn a few yards farther into cover, hiding among the gardeners' delicately concealed tools and compost, they might have escaped his notice. But they were at the end of their resources, and

169

having waited too long, they took hands and ran, across the gigantic approach to the gnomon, there to hesitate again in the shelter of the stone walls, waiting to see him pass them on the path he had chosen. He did not pass. He had seen them flash across the open in their unmistakable blue and white, and had lingered slyly under the sheer face of the tower, edging his way round to the other side, from which they would not be expecting him.

Aware of their nakedness, they had stopped to creep into the first steps of the great staircase, hoping to be hidden from either side. It was the worst thing they could have done. Suddenly he was there, not ten yards away from them, poised to intercept them whichever way they ran; and in order to run at all they had first to break free from the low, containing walls, for they were crouching some few steps from the ground.

Reason no longer had any part in what they did. There was only one way they could retreat from him and remain out of reach, and there was no power left in either of them to reckon for how long. Every moment free of his grasp counted. They bargained only for that, seconds of freedom; beyond there was nothing certain. As he lurched towards the foot of the staircase they scrambled to their feet and ran from him, frantically, frenziedly, up the steps with all the breath and all the muscular force they had, utterly reckless of things which in any other circumstances would have halted them with horror. There was just room for two people to pass on those steps. The walls at the sides scarcely reached their knees. The gradient, though of this they had no idea, was approximately one in two. Below, there was nothing but hot white concrete waiting to receive them. They looked up, and nowhere else. Nothing else was possible. There was not a single person moving, up or down, on all those white steps, except themselves. There was no one warily circling the stone drum on the summit. There was no one left in the world but themselves, and the man who had begun, with hideous leisureliness, to follow them up the gnomon.

170

There was no railing, there on top. Thousands of unsuspecting children climbed these stairs every year, how many played too confidingly around the stone drum on the top? It was nearly as tall as a man, taller than these two girls. Parents might lose sight of their daring offspring, it needed only a little scuffle – children have no idea of danger. How thoughtful of them, how thoughtful, to provide this way out! One of them or both, what did it matter? If the vital one went, the other would be too terrified to cause any further trouble. She was, after all, his elder brother's posthumous daughter. And she had no money, no allies, no power ... not like the other one. No, let Amrita keep her if it worked out that way. Why not? Neither of them would ever dare to point a finger at him. As for him, that other, how easy to give orders and sit back and stay immune! Let him do what he liked, he had no weapons that would not turn against himself. Next time let him do his own dirty work, and find his way out of his own traps. This was the last time Govind Das meant to carry another man's burden!

And no one following up here. No one. Perfect!

He might have to carry Shantila down the steps. No matter, she would not be any trouble, once the other was gone. That one, with her fine clothes, and her confidence, and her way of looking that was not Indian, not Western, but something between, something unique, a manner all her own, native and strange – everywhere native, everywhere strange. He wondered about that parentage of hers. He had never seen her sire. That had been a weakness, for surely she was her father's daughter.

They were slowing now, blown and aching from the long, steep climb. Take it easily now, there must be no violent action to be seen on the skyline here, nothing but gentleness, nothing but family affection suddenly ruptured by tragedy. He could not look down now, he was too high. Fifty feet can seem so much more, without a handrail, with only two feet of level ground between you and space.

171

Slowly, step by step, there was no haste, since there was no way out.

On the last few stairs they were reeling and fumbling with exhaustion, and the man was only a few steps behind. Anjli groped her way ahead, one hand reaching back for Shantila's hand, but often missing it, sweat running down into her eyebrows and lashes, stinging her lips, sickening her. Only to put that stone cone between herself and her enemy, even if there was nothing to hold by, and no way of evading him in the end. Her cleanness, her personality, depended on eluding his touch. There were no other ambitions left to her.

She saw as in a dream the marvellous panorama of Jai Singh's vision from this altitude, and the quiet stretch of Parliament Street outside the wall, beyond the silvery palms. She saw the ripe, rosy fruit at her feet, hemmed with flowers, and the mysterious castle towers behind, spinning on their white central columns, dovecotes for stars. Then, only just behind her, she heard Shantila stumble and fall, clinging to the edge of the step, sobbing with frustration. She turned, reaching to help her up; and past the little heaving body her enemy stepped triumphantly, a hand already reaching out for her.

Shantila saw in the corner of her eye the deliberate foot climbing past her, saw it poised to touch the step above, saw the confident, greedy hand extended. With all the strength she had left she clenched both her hands in the string of her necklace, and tugged the cord apart. A sharp stab of pain seared her throat, beads of blood sprang along the wound and spilled among the Scottish beads. The pebbles from the Cairngorms spurted and danced across the white steps, bouncing, twirling, hard and round and adamant, merry as marbles in a game and double as dangerous. She heard them ring tiny, hard, gay notes of music, cannoning off one another, diverting one another, filling the whole width of the staircase with the irresponsible gaiety of murder. She actually saw Govind Das set his foot squarely

172

upon no less than three of them. But it was the easy leaning forward, the disarrangement of his weight, which actually disposed of him.

The beads rolled, seeking a way downwards, safe enough in any fall. They spilled him forward on his face; his feet went out from under him, and the hand reaching confidently for Anjli's arm missed by inches, and groped helplessly upon the air, baulked of any resting place. He tried to swing his weight and recover his balance, and the only effect was to turn him towards the abyss from which he had climbed, and fling him face-forwards into it. He hurtled past Shantila on the downward road, and she saw his face intent, puzzled, hopeful, still wrestling for balance and incontinent after life, a young man's face incredulous of disaster, certain of salvation. But afraid, afraid, inhumanly afraid! Shantila was fortunate, for she had no terms in which to describe what she had seen, and no one was ever going to demand of her that she should find words for it. It is possible to forget what you have never formulated.

As for Anjli, she never saw it. All she saw was the beads rolling, the foot betrayed, the balance lost, and all this in a moment of time. She stood frozen, unable to withdraw from the hand which nevertheless failed utterly to touch her. From stair to stair, derisively, the Cairngorm pebbles rolled inviolable, skittishly evading every attempt Govind Das made to recover his equilibrium. From stair to stair they bounced happily, like water seeking their own level, oblivious of the plunging, lurching feet that fought in vain for a firm foothold. And after a moment he outran his destroyers, lunging, falling, leaping endlessly downwards, first running, then rolling, then bouncing like a thrown ball, then tossed like a rag-doll, arms and legs flying, bones cracking, an inarticulate thing coursed interminably down the hundred feet of one-in-two slope towards the concrete ground which was the home level, the final goal.

Far down the long white slide the fore-shortened figure of a man had begun to climb after them. They saw him only now, and cried out together in alarm and despair, for

173

how could he possibly evade the grotesque projectile that was hurtling down upon him? He had come too far up the steps to be able to retreat and leap out of the way. He threw himself down, flattened along the stairs with braced feet under the one bordering wall, an arm flung over the rim to anchor him. Nothing could now have arrested the flight of Govind Das. His flailing body struck the tensed bow of Girish's shoulders, and rebounded on to the crest of the opposite wall, sliding helplessly down it for several feet before the uncontrolled weight dragged it over the edge, to fall with a dull half-liquid sound on the bone-white concrete below.

Girish took his head out of his arms, and levered himself up from the steps. There was no more sound from below, and no more movement.

'Be careful!' called Anjli's anxious voice from above him. 'The beads ... on the stairs ...'

Then he saw them, one by one gently trickling down towards their own level, unbruised, adamant, the coloured pebbles from the mountains at the other end of the world. He met and passed them on his way upwards, and gathered the ones that came most easily to hand, so that no one else should mount here and accidentally follow Govind Das to his death. But many eluded him, for all the real passion of his senses and his heart was fixed on the children. Slowly they crept down to meet him, Anjli in front, one hand stretched back to clasp the hand of her friend. She felt her way from step to step with the methodical movements of exhaustion, when you cannot afford a first mistake because it may well be your last. Her face was pale and clear, almost empty as yet because fear had so recently quitted it and left it virgin. Her eyes, immense, so bruised with experience that they might have been darkened with kohl in the native way, clung unwaveringly to his face.

They were above the midway mark when they met. Anjli took her hand gently from Shantila's hand, so that she could join her palms on her breast in the proper reverence.

'Namaste!'

174

He held out his arms, and she walked almost shyly into them, and he kissed her forehead. They came down the steps together all linked in a chain of three, Girish in front for a barrier against any fear they might still feel of lesser things, now that the great fear was gone, Anjli's right hand in his and her left hand in Shantila's. They came slowly, because none of them was in haste now, and none of them was free of the great, clouding lassitude of achievement that hung upon this denouement. They must have heard the voices below, they must have seen the curious gathering at last, too late to be helpful, in time to be in the way. From nowhere someone had conjured two police officers. Through the gates an ambulance was driving. It had failed to find a victim upon the scene of the road accident in Parliament Street, but it would not go back empty-handed from here.

And there were other faces, faces Anjli knew well and some she did not know, but clearly all united in this moment, gathering there at the foot of the steps to welcome her back among them. Dominic, and Tossa, and Mr Felder, all radiant with relief, and an elderly, ascetic gentleman with a saffron robe and a shaven skull and lop-sided spectacles, gently beaming in the background, and an immaculate person in exclusive tailoring, who by his contented smile was clearly also a member of the alliance. She had never realised she had so many friends here. Find one, and you have the key to many more.

Anjli stepped upon solid ground, and her knees trembled under her. The ambulance men were just picking up and screening from sight all that was left of Govind Das.

XII

There were nine of them present in Dominic's hotel sitting-room over coffee that night. The promise made to Ashok had been no vain one, after all; he came straight from a recording session, his head still full of music, to find Anjli, in her own western clothes and with her normal poise rather enhanced than impaired, seated dutifully between Dominic and Tossa, and apparently totally engrossed in pouring coffee for their guests. The Swami Premanathanand sat cross-legged and serene at one end of the cushioned settee, with his driver Girish balancing him at the other end, a silent man with a faint smile and a grazed face, one profile beautiful in a falcon's fashion, the other marred. Felder lay relaxed in a reclining chair, after days of tension. And the last-comers, or so it appeared, surprised everyone, except the Swami, who was not subject to surprise. For Satyavan Kumar did not come alone, but brought with him Kamala, fresh from the expensive salon of Roy and James with her glossy pyramid of black hair heady as a bush of jasmine, and her superb body swathed in a new sari of a miraculous muted shade between lilac and rose and peach. She kissed Anjli, with so serene an implication of divine right that Anjli took no offence, fluttered her fingers at Ashok, and said: 'Darling!' The simplest chair in the room became a throne when she sat in it. 'I should be apologising,' she said, smiling at Dominic, 'I wasn't specifically invited. But I wanted to celebrate, too. I hope you don't mind?'

'I am afraid,' said the Swami, looking modestly down his nose, 'that some of us here are not as well informed about the nature of this – celebration – as the rest. Perhaps first I should explain exactly what has been happening during the last few days.' And he did so, with such admirable brevity that he was done before anyone had breath to comment or question. The only apology, perhaps, is due to you, Mr Kabir. You must forgive your young friend here, it was at my suggestion that he refrained from telling you the truth yesterday. We have not met before, but by sight and by reputation, of course, I know you well, and I assure you it was not from any doubts about you that I excluded you from our counsels. I had a respectable reason, which perhaps will appear later. The invitation to you to join us here tonight was a promise, which you see we have managed to fulfil. I hope it may be taken also as an apology in advance.'

'No one owes me any,' said Ashok. He looked at Anjli, and his sensitive, mobile face pondered in silence the changes in her. 'If this thing had happened, all of us who knew of Anjli's background were suspect. How could I be exempt? You say that Dominic heard and recognised my music ... Kamala's lullaby. Where else should you look, then, but among those of us who knew that music? And we were not so many.'

'Not so many,' agreed the Swami. 'And most of them like Mr Felder here, were in Sarnath at the time of the kidnapping, as you were in Trivandrum, though we did not then know that.'

'*I* was in Delhi,' Kamala said helpfully. 'Yashodhara doesn't appear in the Deer Park scenes. None of the women do. And Subhash Ghose was here, too, and ...'

'And Govind Das,' concluded Felder ruefully.

There was a small, flat silence. 'We hadn't realised,' said Dominic then, 'how many might be left in town. We thought the whole company had moved to Benares. Of course we thought first of the company, but filming in Sarnath seemed to put you all out of the picture. And yet I was always quite certain about Ashok's morning raga. I knew what I'd heard. I'll admit there were times when we didn't know whom we could trust, or even whether we could trust anybody ... even the Swami here. Even you ...' He looked up across the room at the two handsome, smiling people sitting comfortably side by side there, with an almost domestic ease and felicity. 'Last night, Mr Kumar,

177

after you left, Tossa and I were walking round by Claridge's. We saw you leaving together by taxi . . .'

Ashok's eyebrows had soared into his hair. '*Kumar?*' he said half-aloud, astonished and mystified.

Kamala laughed gently. 'Yes, I see that we made difficulties for you. After all these years we still prefer to dine together when we can. Krishan is a serious character actor, I am, let's face it, a fashionable star. Never in our whole married life have we been able to play together in the same film. We are both contrasuggestible. The whole pressure of our work drives us apart. That is why we spend all the time left to us together.'

'Krishan?' Dominic said, confounded.

'*Married* life?' repeated Felder, slowly sitting upright in his chair. 'I didn't even know you *were* married . . .'

'No, darling, of course you didn't. We have a theory. The least publicised marriages are the most durable ones, and we happen to like being married to each other. And after all, you've known me only a little while, and only as one of a company at work.'

'But to *Kumar* here . . .?'

'Oh, no darling, not *Kumar*. How confused you are, I'm so sorry I'm not making myself clear. No, my husband is Krishan Malenkar, and if I may say so, a very good actor indeed. If you should ever be casting a film with an Indian business background, the Swami tells me he made a most appealing, as well as convincing tycoon.'

'But if *he's* not Kumar,' persisted Felder feverishly, 'then *who is?*'

Anjli looked all round the ring of astonished faces, and suddenly rose from her place, unable any longer to subdue the blaze of joy and achievement that shone out of her. She crossed the room to where Girish sat, and put a hand possessively on his shoulder, and he smiled and drew her down beside him.

'*This* is my father,' she said proudly, as if she found it incomprehensible that they could ever have been in doubt.

178

'I knew him as soon as I saw him driving after us. I knew he would come for me.'

All eyes had turned upon the Swami. 'But *why*?' demanded Felder on behalf of them all. 'Why was it necessary to conceal the fact that her father was right here with you? I don't understand what sense it makes.'

'Oh, come!' protested the Swami mildly. 'You do yourself less than justice, Mr Felder, I'm sure. It cannot be so difficult to see a good reason for suppressing Satyavan's identity, since circumstances made it possible. I did not then know which of you, if any, could be trusted. Satyavan, since he left home, has indeed been a law unto himself, and like everyone else, I have seldom known for long where he could be found; but at various times he has been working in several of the Mission's projects, and from time to time I have been in touch with him. At the time of his mother's death I had no idea where to find him, and he did not read the papers regularly, and only learned of her death too late to be present at her funeral rites. As soon as he did hear, he came. To me! We drove together to his house, it was his intention to begin at once to set his affairs in order. You,' he said, turning his mild, bright eyes upon Dominic and Tossa, 'know what we heard and saw when we came to Rabindar Nagar. Should I then have produced him and named him to you, whom we did not know, you, who had been in charge of the child and might be involved in her abduction? No! It was the strength of Satyavan's position that he had not been seen in Rabindar Nagar for more than a year, that many of his neighbours were new, that he returned now straight from the field, not a Delhi businessman but weather-beaten and dressed for work, and driving the Mission car ... He wished to remain in the background, unknown and free to move as he would, for it was *his* daughter who was at risk. From that moment, therefore, we watched you in everything you did, and equally all those who had contact with you. It seemed that any demands for ransom must come through you, and so it turned out. And

179

after the first payment failed to produce Anjli, I judged it necessary to provide another father, a convincing father of the right type, and to have him emerge into the limelight and take charge.'

'But why?' insisted Felder. 'I still don't see the purpose of it.'

'Oh, a very specific purpose. His job was to insist on seeing Anjli alive before more money was paid. For, you see, until then we had no means whatever of being sure that she had not been killed. Yes, yes, Mr Felder, you were horrified at that suggestion, I know, nevertheless it is common form in these cases. But when my good friend Malenkar played his scene, insisted on seeing with his own eyes – and incidentally with ours, too! – that she still lived, *and when there was no demur*, then we had a certain degree of security. A fairly substantial degree, in fact. Enough to make plans. For Satyavan, apparently a servant, and therefore virtually invisible, was free to observe and to act. On his behalf no one ever made any bargains. These are my reasons for acting as I did. Was it well done?'

'*Yes!*' said Dominic and Tossa together fervently. '*Very* well done!'

'And that is why I could not let Mr Kabir come upstairs and join us here last night. I cannot say whether he actually knows Satyavan by sight, though I thought it a possibility. But I *did* know that he is very well acquainted with Malenkar, and would most probably have given the show away on the spot.'

'*To which one of us?*' Dominic asked very gently.

The Swami's mild eyes sharpened upon him almost alarmingly, if there had not been in the brief, brilliant glance a suggestion of distinct approval.

'Ah, I did not then know of the activities of Govind Das. I was still acting on the assumption that the director of the affair might be any one of you. It seems now that the whole thing was planned and carried out by this one man.'

'A bad business,' said Felder soberly.

'As you say, a bad business. It turned out so for him.'

180

'Small part actors don't make much money. Probably here they don't get to many parts, either. Or anywhere, for that matter, these days. I suppose seeing temptation trailed in front of his nose like that was too much for him – the daughter of a milllionaire and a film star, and only two students new to India taking care of her. It must have looked easy! Well, thank goodness it's over! The poor wretch who planned and did it is dead. He's paid. That's the end of it.'

A long, communicated sigh went round the room, and subsided into a deep and thoughtful silence.

'Except,' said Anjli suddenly, erect and sombre by her father's side, '*if* he did it all alone, why did Shantila say *they'd told him* not to hurt me? That's what she said. Tomorrow you can ask her.'

A curious flutter of uneasiness stirred the air.

'And *if* he did it all alone,' Dominic said slowly, 'then he must be a genius, to be able to come up with that scheme about lunch at Sawyers' and a taxi to the sweet shop opposite, the very minute he was faced with having to arrange a way of letting us see Anjli. Now if he'd already been primed by somebody who *knew* what was going to happen . . .'

'And what,' wondered Tossa, 'if he *did* do it all alone, what has he done with the money from the first payment we made at the Birla temple? Because you know what the police said – they haven't found a trace of it at his house or in his sister-in-law's quarters at the office.'

'And if it wasn't he who took the money from the briefcase,' supplemented the Swami, warming to the theme, 'then who was it? And where is it now? It would be so much more satisfactory, would it not, to recover it? Even film stars who *do* make a great deal of money should not be made the victims of extortion.'

'They certainly shouldn't,' agreed Felder warmly. 'I've still got to justify that to Dorrie, but at least she still has a daughter, thank God. It does seem a pity, but it hardly looks as if we'll ever see that money again.'

'Oh, do not lose heart,' the Swami encouraged him benignly. 'Perhaps, after all, there is still hope that the police may discover it somewhere.'

'Well, if they do, presumably there may be some hope of deducing how it got there. Until then I'm afraid we haven't much chance.'

And indeed it seemed that it was over, and that there was no longer anything to hold them all here together; yet no one made any move to go. It was almost as if they were waiting for something to happen which would release them and let them fly apart again into their proper orbits, Dominic and Tossa, tired, relieved and infinitely grateful, back to England, the Swami to the minute office from which he pulled so many valiant and unexpected strings in the life of unprivileged India, Krishan Malenkar and his Kamala to their well-guarded private life, Anjli wherever her new father led her, deeper and deeper into the complex soul of this sub-continent, Ashok back to the cosmic solitude where the great artists create their own companions, like self-generating gods; and Felder . . .

Someone rapped at the door, briskly, quietly and with absolute authority.

'Come in!' called Dominic.

Inspector Kulbir Singh came in with aplomb. His black beard was tucked snugly into its retaining net, his moustache was immaculately waxed at the ends, which turned up in military fashion to touch his bold cheek-bones. In his hands – gloved hands – he held a large, fat bank envelope, linen-grained, biscuit-coloured. Every eye in the room fastened on it, and for an instant everyone held his breath.

'Ladies . . . Swami . . . gentlemen, forgive this intrusion. There is a small matter of identification with which you can help me, if you will.' He came forward with assurance, and laid the envelope upon the coffee table, drawing out delicately wad after wad of notes. 'No, no, please do not touch. There is the question of finger prints. I would ask you only to look at this packet . . . you, Mr Felder, Mr Felse and Miss Barber. The total amount, you may take my word, is

182

two hundred thousand rupees, as you see in notes of various values. It is contained in an envelope of the State Bank of India, issued at the branch here in Parliament Street. Their stamp bears last Saturday's date. I must ask you if you can identify this package.'

They stood staring all three, alike stricken into silence. Dominic was the first to clear his throat. 'It looks very like the money Mr Felder drew from the bank, in my presence, on Saturday morning. The amount is right.'

'Miss Barber?'

'I wasn't at the bank. I saw the package the next day, when Mr Felder left it at the desk, downstairs. This one looks the same. I feel sure it is. There was a linen thread half an inch too long, projecting out of that left corner of the flap, just like that one. My prints should be on the envelope, if it's the same one. I collected it from the desk, and Dominic put it into the briefcase.'

'Thank you, that is very helpful. Mr Felder? Does it appear the same to you?'

'I can't be sure. One bank envelope is very like another. It could be the same.'

'Even to the amount inside it, Mr Felder?'

'I've said, it could be the same.'

'In that case your prints should also be on the envelope, I take it, since you handled it.'

'Yes, certainly I did. I kept it safe until I delivered it to this hotel on Sunday morning.'

'But you would not expect your prints also to be on the notes?'

'Of course not, why should they be? I took the package from the bank teller intact, and as you know, it was paid over to Miss Kumar's kidnapper at the Birla temple on Sunday afternoon.' He raised his head, and stared Inspector Singh stonily in the eyes. 'Where did you find it?'

'In a locked suitcase in a room in the Villa Lakshmi at Hauz Khas, Mr Felder – the bedroom occupied by you.'

Felder drew back from him a long pace; all the deep,

183

easy-going lines of his face had sagged into grey pallor.

'You know what this is, don't you? A plant to leave me holding the baby. Yes, I drew the money, yes, I handled the parcel, that you know already from all of us, what have I got to deny? We paid that money over at the temple, as we were told to do. There was a parcel of sliced-up newsprint left in its place, and that we've told you, too, it isn't any secret. But if you think I made that exchange, think again. Kumar here was watching me all that afternoon. He knows I never went near the place where the briefcase was.' He swung on Satyavan, who sat unmoved, his arm round his daughter, his grazed cheek seamed with darkening scars beneath the levelled black eye. 'Tell him! You were watching me as I was watching the briefcase. You came and started talking to me, and that cost us – how many minutes? Three? Enough for the exchange to be made. I wasn't watching during those few minutes, and neither were you.'

'That is true, Inspector,' said Satyavan. 'I spoke to him. For perhaps as long as three minutes he was not watching the case, and neither was I.'

'*But I was,*' said the Swami's voice, with infinite gentleness and absolute certainly.

Everyone turned, almost cautiously, as though he might vanish if they were too abrupt. He sat relaxed and tranquil, his face fixed in a slight and rueful smile, and all the reflected light in the room had gathered in a highlight on his golden shoulder, like a lantern set in the protruding bone.

'Yes, I, too, was present. Satyavan and I had been following your movements and those of these young people ever since the murder and the abduction of the child. Satyavan came and spoke to you because he believed you had noticed him, and suspected his interest in you. But as it appeared, his approach was welcome and useful to you. Yes! But all that time I was sitting in meditation on the terrace of the temple. No one finds it strange that such as I should sit and meditate, even for long periods, even upon something so mundane as a briefcase and two pairs of shoes. No, it is perfectly true, you did not go near them in all that

184

time. That I confirm. *But neither did anyone else!*'

The silence waited and grew, allowing them time to grasp that and understand what it meant.

'From the moment when this boy placed it there to the moment when he took it up again, no one touched it. Therefore it was, when placed, exactly as it was when removed, filled only with newsprint. The ransom – the first ransom – had been collected in advance. By you! Miss Lester would have repaid it to the company without a qualm, would she not, since it was employed in her daughter's interest?'

Felder opened his dry lips, and tried to speak, but made no sound.

'Even film directors, Mr Felder, do not always make enough money for their needs, and cannot resist temptation when it walks across their path. It is a question rather of the moderation and control of one's needs. Of the conquest of desire. But your desires were clearly immoderate. Therefore, when you could not resist retaining Anjli in the hope of further easy gain, we placed before you the bait of a second and greater ransom, to discover whether she was still safe, and to ensure that you would keep her so.'

'What do you take me for?' Felder had found his voice now, it burst out full and strong with genuine indignation. 'I wouldn't have hurt a hair of her head. I always meant to give her back safe and sound. What do you think I am? I may have needed money, I may have taken short cuts, but Dorrie's girl wasn't expendable.'

'No,' agreed the Swami, with deep sadness. 'No, the half-American child, *your friend's* child, was not expendable to you. You gave your accomplice his orders to keep her safe, not to hurt her ... of course, you are a humane man, you did not kidnap or kill – *not in the first person, only by proxy*. When you hired him, did you ask him how he meant to carry out his coup? Did you tell him, no violence to anyone? No, you shut your ears and left it to him. He was paid, was he not? A wisp of Indian dust, an old, decrepit creature, a beggar, hardly a man at all to you – *Arjun Baba was expendable*!'

185

'Let us, however, be realistic,' observed the Swami, breaking the long silence which had descended on the room after Ernest Felder had been taken away. 'He cannot be charged with the murder of Arjun Baba. Quite certainly he did not commit that crime himself, and with Govind Das dead it will be almost impossible to prove that it arose as a direct result of the conspiracy Felder inspired. Indeed, I doubt if they will ever be able to charge him with the abduction, unless he is foolish enough to repeat the virtual confession we have just heard. Govind Das cannot convict him, and I doubt if Mrs Das ever so much as heard his name mentioned. Probably the only charge they can hope to bring home is of the misappropriation of that company money.'

'There is also something to be said,' Satyavan said softly, 'even for Felder.' Anjli's eyes were drooping into sleep, and her head was heavy on his shoulder. 'My wife was indebted to him for all her early chances in films. He is not the only one of whom she has made use when it suited her, and forgotten for years in between, but perhaps he was the most complaisant. If she wanted to send Anjli here to me, it would be quite natural to her to look round and see who might be useful to her in the matter. Ernest is filming in Delhi? How convenient! Of course, get him to meet the party and do whatever is necessary. He always had complied, why should he let her down now? She is now much more successful, much more wealthy than he, but she still asks, and he still complies. She put the opportunity into his hands, perhaps even the temptation into his mind. It may well have seemed to him that she owed him far more than he meant to extort from her. And am I not partially guilty? I do not believe he decided to act until I failed to come to the aid of both my mother and my child, and left her an easy prey. It's too deep for me. Maybe justice will have to find its own way to every one of us in its own time. I have no doubt it will arrive in the end.'

'It has caught up already,' said Ashok gently, 'with you.' And he caught the drowsy eye Anjli had just re-opened, and made a faun's face at her. 'Have you forgotten? When

Yashodhara bore a child, the Lord Buddha cried: "It must be named Rahula. For a fetter is fastened upon me this day!"'

'I shall call you Rahula,' said Satyavan, tightening his arm about his daughter, 'when you most tyrannise over me.'

Anjli smoothed her cheek against his shoulder like a kitten, and smiled. 'Rahula was a boy. Girls are different. The Lord Buddha should have had a girl.' She looked up at him, suddenly grave and momentarily wide-awake. 'What will happen to Shantila's mother? She was good to me. As good as she dared be.'

'Be easy, my Rahula! No charge will ever be made against Mrs Das with my support. If she had not had a daughter, I should now have been searching in vain for mine.'

'And Shantila?'

'Shantila is your sister, and therefore my child. We must find a safe job for the mother, and she shall be always with you, if you want her.'

'Yes, please, I do want her. We ought to buy her another necklace,' she said indistinctly, 'in place of the one she broke.'

'That is very true,' he said, drawing her more securely into his arm, for she was half asleep. 'Remind me!' He looked up over her head at Dominic and Tossa, and said in a glowing whisper: 'It is late, I shall take her away with me. But tomorrow, wait for us, we shall come to fetch you to Rabindar Nagar.'

They protested dutifully that their job was done now, that they must make their preparations for going home.

'Not yet, not until you must. You will be her guests, she will be happy harrying Kishan Singh to make everything ready for you. Do you not see that my mother Purnima left a true Indian matriarch to be her heiress? I have resigned my life to this creature.' By then she was fast asleep in his arms. 'Ashok, I must warn you, for I see that she may well demand that I propose a match with you – she will have no

187

dowry, she has been urging me to give away everything I have.'

It was past midnight, and they had hardly marked the hours slipping by. When they went out by the balcony to the garden stairs, the stars were lacquered in thick coruscations over the velvet Delhi sky, and there was the shimmer and purity of frost in the air. One by one, a procession massed reverently about Anjli asleep on her father's shoulder, they went down the white steps, and issued with shadows for sails upon the white, paved ocean of the patio.

'At this same hour, I think,' said Satyavan, whispering over his daughter's head, 'I got up in Rabindar Nagar, and found, like the Lord Buddha himself, that the gods had filled the universe with the thought that it was time to go forth.'

'Where?' asked Dominic, hypnotised.

'That is of secondary importance. What matters is to leave what has always been, and look for what has never been yet. I had had riches and marriage and a child, and I had nothing. Nothing is not enough for any man. The only answer is to abandon that nothing, and go in search of something. A different kind of treasure, perhaps. A different kind of salvation. Perhaps not salvation at all, only the loss of oneself.'

'What will you do now?'

'My cousin – you hardly know him – he is a good fellow, he will enjoy living in my mother's house and managing my mother's companies. He will make money, but not want to keep it. As for me, in the past year I have become half a soil scientist and half a stock-breeder. What this Rahula of mine will become I cannot yet guess. I told you, she is encouraging me to put everything I have into the missions. Nobody knows yet what *she* has to put into them. I am afraid it may be more than I can command. We have a whole sub-continent to grow into, she and I. Tomorrow,' he said, with deep content, 'you will come and join us.'

'No – you've only just discovered each other —'

'We have a lifetime,' said Satyavan, breathing in the

night, 'and you have return tickets valid for weeks yet. When does your new term begin?'

'Come,' said the Swami, waiting by the door of the Rolls, 'would you like me to drive you?'

Just now the stars must be nesting in the niches of the magic towers at the Jantar Mantar, like doves coming home to their cotes.

'Good night!' whispered Malenkar, holding the door of their car for his wife.

'Good bye!' breathed Kamala. 'Ashok, can we give you a lift?'

'I'll send you a recording of the music,' promised Ashok, and touched the butterfly ribbon of Anjli's plait as her father lifted her gently into the Rolls, among the grain-sacks and the experimental feed. She breathed lightly and long, smiling on his shoulder. She had everything in the world she wanted, and she was never going to look back.

'Tomorrow . . . ten o'clock!' whispered Satyavan.

The Malenkar Mercedes drew away first, the lofty Rolls proceeding majestically after. The two of them were left alone in the silence bone-white with moonight. The un-uttered notes floated silently across the pale space and nested in the tall hedge behind which the cars had vanished.

'Raga Aheer Bhairab,' said Tossa in the softest of under-tones. 'To be played in the early hours of the morning . . .'

'. . . when the guests are departing . . .'